"You ask a lot of just a kiss."

"See, that's the point," she said. "It should never be 'just a kiss.' And if we didn't offer them to all and sundry, but just to those for whom we feel something, they would be special."

Gib's challenge remained in place. "Then you don't want the kiss?"

He was giving the little virgin a graceful out—and she didn't want it.

"I didn't say that." She took a step toward him and saw surprise in the depths of his eyes. "You don't mind my being in charge?"

He took a step toward her. "No one's in charge," he corrected. "It's a mutual communication."

"Do you want to change your mind?"

"No."

She almost hoped he'd say yes. Then she remembered that she was trying to make a point.

She looped her arms around his neck. His hands came up gently to her shoulder blades. She lifted her mouth toward him and watched, her heart thudding, as he lowered his head to meet her lips....

ABOUT THE AUTHOR

Muriel Jensen and her husband, Ron, live in Astoria, Oregon in an old Four-Square Victorian at the mouth of the Columbia River. They share their home with a golden retriever/golden Labrador mix named Amber, and five cats who moved in with them without an invitation. (Muriel insists that a plate of Friskies and a bowl of water are not an invitation!)

The couple has three children and their families in their lives—a veritable crowd of the most interesting people and children. They also have irreplaceable friends, wonderful neighbors and "a life they know they don't deserve but love desperately anyway."

Books by Muriel Jensen

HARLEQUIN AMERICAN ROMANCE

119—LOVERS NEVER LOSE
176—THE MALLORY TOUCH
200—FANTASIES & MEMORIES
219—LOVE AND LAVENDER
244—THE DUCK SHACK AGREEMENT
267—STRINGS
283—SIDE BY SIDE
321—A CAROL CHRISTMAS
339—EVERYTHING
392—THE MIRACLE
414—RACING WITH THE MOON
425—VALENTINE HEARTS AND FLOWERS
464—MIDDLE OF THE RAINBOW
478—ONE AND ONE MAKES THREE
507—THE UNEXPECTED GROOM
522—NIGHT PRINCE
534—MAKE-BELIEVE MOM
549—THE WEDDING GAMBLE
569—THE COURTSHIP OF DUSTY'S DADDY
603—MOMMY ON BOARD
606—MAKE WAY FOR MOMMY
610—MERRY CHRISTMAS, MOMMY!
654—THE COMEBACK MOM
669—THE PRINCE, THE LADY & THE TOWER
688—KIDS & CO.
705—CHRISTMAS IN THE COUNTRY
737—DADDY BY DEFAULT
742—DADDY BY DESIGN
746—DADDY BY DESTINY
756—GIFT-WRAPPED DAD

The Hunk & the Virgin

MURIEL JENSEN

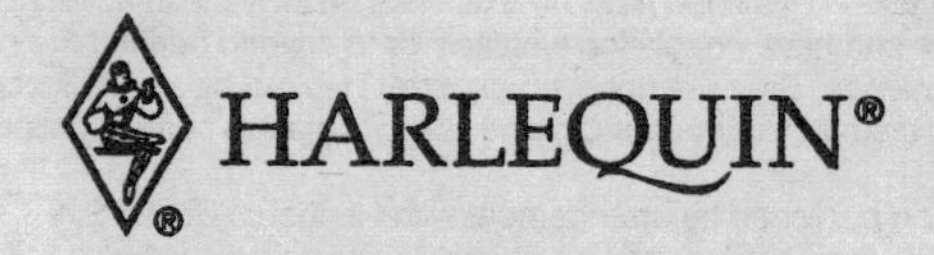

TORONTO • NEW YORK • LONDON
AMSTERDAM • PARIS • SYDNEY • HAMBURG
STOCKHOLM • ATHENS • TOKYO • MILAN • MADRID
PRAGUE • WARSAW • BUDAPEST • AUCKLAND

To Robert, Warren and Joan Jensen,
the best in-laws anyone ever had.

ISBN 0-373-16770-9

THE HUNK & THE VIRGIN

This edition published by arrangement with Harlequin Books S.A.

Printed in U.S.A.

Chapter One

Gib London turned away from his computer to frown at the women gathered around his desk. They looked like Cary Grant's aunts in *Arsenic and Old Lace,* except that there were three of them. They wore wire-rimmed eyeglasses, silky flowered dresses with hand-crocheted collars and their gray hair in tidy little buns. His aunts were lovable and charming but prone to eccentricities that often threatened their small publishing firm and therefore his position there.

"You want me to what?" he asked, certain he'd misunderstood.

Cordelia, the tallest, the eldest and the most forceful, repeated the order with which they'd walked into his office a moment ago. "We want you to serve as a bodyguard on one of our author tours."

"*One* of our author tours?" Rose, the youngest sister and the one into details, rolled her bright blue eyes. "In twenty-seven years in the business, this is the *only* author tour we've ever had."

Lucinda, the family historian, raised a long, slender finger. "Since we've had ownership of London Publishing, that's true. But father sent David Bromwell on a tour in 1946. The war hero. You remember."

Cordelia nodded with a sharp glance at the middle sister. "Of course we remember. You and he had to be dragged back from Las Vegas, and you, Rose and I were in solitary confinement for weeks because of your antics."

Lucinda sighed wistfully, then refocused on her sisters. "My point was, there *has* been another tour."

The bickering began again, but Gib stopped it with a firm "Ladies!" He stood to put Cordelia in his chair. Then he seated Rose and Lucinda on the horizontal file cabinet against the wall. If he didn't get their attention, they would quarrel and nitpick like the spoiled young heiresses they'd been in the forties.

Because of a domineering and overprotective father, Gib's aunts never married and were now simply remnants of another time, sharing custody of a publishing company that had been one of the giants, but was now holding on by its fingernails to a small share of the market.

But they didn't really care about their reduced circumstances. They had their memories and the ability to buy any manuscript that struck their fancies or appealed to their outdated concepts of family life.

They'd invited him onboard last year when their business manager walked out in the middle of contract negotiations. Gib had just left a comfortable job with Crawford House, looking for...well, he wasn't sure what he'd been looking for, only that he hadn't found it.

He loved his aunts dearly, but being in their company wasn't conducive to the clear thought and sharp focus he thought might be needed to discover just what it was he was missing.

"You're not sending the butterfly book on tour?" he asked Cordelia.

She shook her head. He turned to Rose. "The five hundred rhubarb recipes?"

"Of course not," Rose replied.

"Aunt Lucy. The genealogy-search-via-computer book?"

Lucinda replied, "No, dear."

Oh, no, he thought. *Don't let it be.* The only other title in the hopper for holiday release was the one he'd advised them not to buy—the one he'd considered even more outdated than his aunts, the one they'd bought, anyway.

He sank onto the corner of his desk. "You're sending that little redheaded virgin on tour," he said dismally, sensing the impending doom of London Publishing.

Rose came to put an arm around his shoulders. She stood only slightly taller than his sitting position and smelled of the flower after which she'd been named. "It's something we understand, Gilbert," she said gently. "And something we believe in. We're old, but we still feel very connected to the women of our world. We want the next generation coming up to know they have choices that aren't very visible to them in our society."

He caught her arms in a desperate attempt to make her listen to him. "Aunt Rose." He looked at Cordelia, then at Lucinda. "All of you. Please. Listen." He struggled to find a diplomatic way of expressing the truth they had to hear. "You know I love you very much."

They nodded in unison, giving him three loving smiles in return.

"You more than proved that," Lucinda said, "when you came to work for us instead of taking that six-figure offer from Browning Books."

He'd since seriously wondered at the wisdom of responding with his heart instead of his head. It wasn't a choice he usually made, but when he'd been a boy, these women had given him the love and attention his globe-trotting parents had been too busy to provide.

"Then, please listen to me," he said quietly. "I know you believe in this McQuade woman's book because it's familiar to you. It says all the things you were taught as girls. But, Aunts, the world's a very different place today. You don't get out in it that much, so you don't see it, but man-woman relationships are very different than they used to be. Asking young men and women to abstain from sex for years while they pursue careers, or suggesting that they marry just to have it is...is..." He couldn't come up with a word that defined the absurdity of the concept as he saw it. So he attacked from another direction. "I told you when you bought the book, and I'm telling you now, Aunts. It's going to bomb, big-time. And if you add tour costs to production costs, we're going to be lucky to survive the year."

They looked appropriately grave. They always did their best to humor him.

Except Cordelia. She stood and came around the desk to him, unfolding a sheet of paper from her pocket and offering it for his inspection. "Look at these sales, Mr. Marriage-is-for-Misfits. And they're still coming in.''

Gib read the column of figures and the names of the book vendors who'd ordered—and reordered—in astonishingly large numbers.

Lucinda came to stand beside her sister. ''You wouldn't listen to us,'' she said, reading over his shoulder, ''when we told you there's a considerable movement toward celibacy in young people. They're no less horny than they used to be, they're just getting some smarts.''

''Lucy!'' said Rose. ''Must you be so vulgar?'' Rose patted Gib's shoulder. ''The world's in a mess, Gilbert. And while London Publishing can't effect big changes, we can affect one young person at a time by making available to them what Kathryn McQuade has to say.''

He got to his feet and smiled down at them, clustered around his shoulders. ''Then, maybe it's time for us to part company. You have every right to espouse what you believe, but before I align myself with the bigoted moralists and judgmental—''

Lucinda had gone to his bookshelf and pulled down a review copy of *The Virgin Returns.* She handed it to him. ''Did you ever read this as we asked you to?''

He took it from her. ''No, I haven't.''

She smiled sweetly at him. ''Then, doesn't that make you just a bigoted moralist of another sort?''

It probably did, but before he admitted that, he tried once more to make them see the flaw in their theory.

''How many times,'' he asked, ''has my father—your brother—been married?''

His aunts looked at each other. "Four," Cordelia replied.

"And my convent-educated mother?"

That look again. Rose answered for them. "Three."

"All right," he said, looking from one upturned face to the next. "Seven broken marriages, all in a search for love." He said the word with the scorn he'd learned to give it after a succession of stepparents had paraded through his life. "What is the point in saving yourself for someone who turns out not to be who you thought he or she was at all?"

Cordelia opened her mouth to reply, but he prevented her by answering the question himself. "In the interest of your own good health—yes, I know. But there are protections in place for that, and a little discrimination would allow you a little comfort in your bed."

Lucinda opened her mouth as though to offer a rebuttal, then seemed to change her mind. She tapped the book he still held. "I think you should read this, Gibby." Then she took it from him, turned it over so that the portrait of the author on the back was uppermost and handed it back to him. "I memoed you about this, but I don't know if you remember. This manuscript began as her thesis for her master's in psychology, so we're not dealing with an hysterical, uninformed dummy."

Rose hugged him affectionately. "Unless we're talking about you. 'Bye, dear. We have a lunch date with the Bookish rep. Did you notice how many books they bought?"

Gib stood in place, speechless, as his aunts

trooped out of his office. Then a sudden thought occurred to him and he shouted, "Wait!"

His aunts turned in a group at the doorway.

"Why would she need a bodyguard?" he asked.

Cordelia closed her eyes as though the reason caused her great distress. "We sent press releases to all the media, including, of course, radio stations. Harold Morganstern talked about the book on his show this morning."

Harold Morganstern, Gib knew, was a talk-show host with off-the-wall guests and outrageous and even antisocial opinions on everything. Half the population hated him, including Gib, but everyone listened to him.

"He said," Cordelia continued, "if a beautiful woman like Kathy remains virginal at twenty-six, then the men of this country are either asleep or unconscious."

"He issued a challenge," Lucinda said, "to all the single young men across the country to charm Kathy into changing her mind."

"*Charm* was the operative word, mercifully," Rose added. "But we all know that charm can be deadlier than force to our convictions. But also, we just want her to be safe. So, you're to keep those young men at bay throughout the tour."

"Aunt Cordie," he implored. "I'm your entire financial department. I can't go chasing from city to city after your little virgin for four weeks when we're on the edge of ruin!"

Cordelia patted his cheek. "This book is going to save us, Gib, so we're pulling out all the stops. It's your job to save her for us. Read the book, darling. We really have to go."

As his aunts left his office, a sense of dread inched up from Gib's toes to tighten right where Kathryn McQuade thought he and single men like him shouldn't see any activity.

Mercy.

He studied the face smiling up at him from the back of *The Virgin Returns.* She looked like Nicole Kidman—a pretty, sharply defined gamine face with wide, light blue eyes that seemed to suggest she knew more than her stand on sex should allow.

A curly cloud of carroty hair lent her an air of innocence that was also curiously sophisticated. Like that look in her eyes.

He'd known many women in his lifetime, some of them very complex. But he thought of innocence and sophistication as defining standards; women were usually one or the other. Never both at the same time.

Except this one. At least by the look of her.

Was one look genuine and the other a mask? A trick? A game?

He walked around his desk to sit in his chair, prop his feet on the old oak desktop, and open the book, determined that no one would deceive his aunts as long as he drew breath.

KATHRYN MCQUADE WAS on her sixth mile on the treadmill when a hand bearing a fluffy white towel was inserted between her face and the tiny built-in television. Oprah vanished in a square of white terry cloth.

"Time to stop torturing yourself," Patsy McQuade said loudly over the hum of the machine, "and look at what I bought you to wear on tour."

Kathy stepped lightly off the belt onto the sides of the treadmill and turned it off.

"I thought we had agreed that we weren't going to buy anything new, Mom." Kathy stepped off the machine, pressing the towel to her face and throat. "The tour's supposed to help us make money, not serve as a reason to spend it."

Patsy McQuade hit Kathy on the head with a shirt box. Kathy's mother might have been her twin, except for dark brown hair with a few strands of gray and lines at the corners of her eyes that were more flattering than unbecoming. "Oh, don't be such a sobersides. You're going to be a celebrity. You don't want to go on national television looking like a frump, do you?"

Before Kathy could answer that, her mother tore the lid off a dress box and drew out a red wool dress with a rolled collar and a slim skirt. "Isn't this just delicious? And look at this." She opened another box and held up a navy blazer, then two pairs of slacks, one blue, one winter white.

Kathy suppressed an instinctive lust for the beautiful clothes. "Very pretty, Mom, but if you charged them, I want you to take them back."

Patsy spread her arms in frustration. "Kathryn Victoria, what foreign stork delivered you to me, anyway? I'm your mother, you're not mine. And you are not going to spend your life getting me out of debt. This tour is about getting you known as an author!"

Kathy sank into one of two barrel chairs her mother had brought with her when she'd moved in three months ago. If she ignored the fuchsia-and-chartreuse-plaid upholstery, they were really quite comfortable—just not to look at. "No, Mom. This tour is about getting you out of debt and square with the IRS," she said firmly. "Then we'll talk about my career."

Patsy pointed a finger at Kathy. Kathy knew that gesture was a demand for silence and added in blatant defiance, "So, there!"

Patsy threw down the clothes and sat in the other chair. "I'm not going to argue with you now, because stress will make you wrinkle. My debts are my problems."

"Your problem is that you gave Jack Trent a job at the print shop and, I think, maybe even your heart. You trusted him to behave accordingly, and instead he ran off with your car and your bank account!"

Patsy reached across the little table that separated them and caught Kathy's hand. "I keep telling you that I *gave* him the car, and I'm allowed to do what I want with my money. I was tired of keeping the print shop going. Desktop publishing has taken a toll on printers, you know. It's time for me to do something else." She squeezed Kathy's hand and gave her a winning smile. "I appreciate your letting me stay with you while I get on my feet again. And I'll be out of your way as quickly as I can. Now. Do you like the clothes?"

"Mom, I love the clothes. But let's face it. I think the London ladies are being a little optimistic about my book. I wrote my thesis based on genuine findings and developed it into a book because I thought the young people's trend toward celibacy might have created a market for it. I know the Londons are excited about sales so far, but I doubt it's going to be a runaway bestseller, so don't think we're going to make a fortune. You and I are going to be roommates for a good long time.''

Patsy pinched Kathy's fingers punitively. ''I don't care what happens financially, although I'd love to see you make a bundle, but I'm telling you, that won't matter to me because I'm not taking a dime of it. I got a job at the China Cup, and I don't have to start until we get home. I'll get my bills paid. When I dissolved the business, I took care of most of my payables except back taxes. But I'll get to those.''

Kathy passed a hand in front of her mother's eyes as though testing her awareness. ''Which is going to be accumulating interest and penalties at a horrifying rate. Mom, file charges against Jack Trent. Maybe he hasn't spent it all yet, and you can get some of it back.''

''Kathy,'' Patsy said firmly, looking into her eyes. ''He did not take the money. And I don't want to talk about him anymore.'' She smiled brightly. ''I'll get tips. Big tips, because I'm charming. Now, give me a break, Kath. For a month can we just forget that I owe all kinds of money, and that you're a little stuffed shirt? Can we just enjoy traveling and your being the center of attention?''

Kathy took exception to the stuffed-shirt remark. ''I am not—''

''Yes, you are,'' Patsy insisted, getting to her feet and slipping into the blazer. ''You're a little worrywart, and you've been trying to boss me around since your father died.''

''I was only nine when he died.''

''That didn't stop you.'' Patsy wandered out of

the room, apparently in search of a mirror. Kathy followed her.

"You've always thought you were the most responsible of the two of us and that you should be in charge." Patsy went into the tiny bathroom and stood on tiptoe to study her reflection in the medicine cabinet's mirror. She turned and looked at herself over her shoulder. "You've always mistaken laughter and lightheartedness for carelessness."

Kathy stood in the bathroom doorway, and Patsy stopped her fashion inspection to touch Kathy's cheek. "I think it's because you adored your father and always wanted to be just like him."

Kathy decided that was probably true. She could still remember the comfort and sense of security his presence brought her.

"He was wonderful," Patsy went on, "but so serious. He should have had more fun. Just like you. All you do is work and exercise and write."

"I'm happy," Kathy insisted. "And someday I'm going to sell a great mystery series. I just have to support myself as a bookstore clerk in the meantime."

"You're content," Patsy corrected. "That's not the same thing. Nice, but not the same. And you'll never know the difference until you find happiness."

Patsy pulled off the blazer and held it for Kathy to slip into.

Kathy obliged. "I'll be happy," she said, "when your debts are paid off, and *you* can be happy."

From behind her, Patsy smiled at Kathy's reflection. "I *am* happy. My life doesn't have to be in perfect order for that. I have you, I have friends, I have a job when we come home..."

Kathy frowned at her mother in the mirror. "You have a friend who deceived you and stole from you."

"I *gave* him the car," Patsy said slowly, as though tired of repeating it.

"And you knew he intended to disappear with it?"

"I knew he had things to do."

"So, you've heard from him?"

Patsy held her daughter's eyes for a moment, then lowered them and sighed. "No. But I expect to."

Kathy could picture Jack Trent, her mother's friend from her days on Bayside's small weekly newspaper before Kathy was even born. He'd returned to Bayside a year ago, thin and looking desperate, and her mother had given him a job in the print shop she and Kathy's father had founded together and that her mother had kept afloat since his death.

Jack had disappeared suddenly three months ago. Almost immediately afterward, Patsy had dissolved the business.

Kathy still felt murderous when she thought about it.

"I think you're angry," Patsy said, "because you liked him, too."

Kathy turned to her mother. "I'm angry because he ruined your life!"

"I assure you my life is not ruined. In fact, I'm very hopeful about the future." Patsy smoothed the shoulders of the blazer. "And yours is just about to take off, so can't we just be happy?"

"Are you going to file charges?"

"No."

"Then I can't be happy. He stole from you! You're letting yourself be a victim."

Patsy looked into Kathy's eyes and for the first time, Kathy saw the pain in her mother's pale gaze.

"He'll be back," her mother said with a little quaver that made her statement less than convincing.

Kathy took hold of her mother's shoulders in exasperation. "Mom, get real! You sound like Pollyanna."

Patsy smiled. "Really. I'm not the one who wrote a book that espouses celibacy in an age where kids are experimenting with sex in middle school."

Kathy struggled to remain reasonable. "I told you the book wouldn't be popular, but I think restraint could change the world, even completely apart from any moral issue. But you know all that. You edited the book for me."

Patsy nodded with self-satisfaction. "Because I believe every Pollyanna has a right to her rainbows on the wall. You're no different from me, you know. You're just a little more serious about it. So don't accuse me of tilting at windmills."

"Pollyanna did not tilt at windmills. You're mixing metaphors."

"You know what I mean. You just don't like to admit it. Come on. Let's try on the dress."

Kathy followed docilely as her mother went back to the spare bedroom. *Saints preserve us!* she thought. *Pollyanna and Don Quixote are going on tour.*

Chapter Two

"Gib! How nice. Now we're all here," Rose said, opening the door to the porch of the fussy old three-story Victorian house she shared with her sisters and pulling Gib into the hall. He wrapped her in an affectionate hug.

The house was just as it had been when the London sisters' grandfather had built it in 1896, complete with Oriental rugs, heavy draperies, lace-covered tables and fussy lamps and curios on every flat surface.

It smelled of dried herbs and lemon oil and the inoffensive must of age. He'd spent a lot of hours in this home as a child, and though its dated extravagance was not an environment in which he would expect to be at ease, it remained synonymous with love and comfort, and so he always felt serene here.

Except for this afternoon.

He'd read Kathryn McQuade's book yesterday as his aunts had insisted and now felt more confused than enlightened. The woman presented solid arguments for celibacy in a logical, coherent and particularly well-written way.

The problem, as he saw it, was that if she did

indeed believe what she said in *The Virgin Returns,* she might very well be laughed off the tour, and the three of them would be stranded somewhere in Poughkeepsie.

If she didn't believe it, then she was a liar and a charlatan, and he would feel as though London Publishing had stolen $18.95 from everyone who bought the book.

He was determined to learn the truth this afternoon.

Rose led him to the parlor, decorated in pink and burgundy with a medallion-backed settee and matching chairs. Lucinda, who always manned the kitchen, had already brought in the tea trolley.

On the other side of it, in the ornately carved bishop's chair Grandfather London had always occupied when he was alive, sat the young woman responsible for his quandary.

Her hair was caught in a curly bunch at the back of her neck so that there was nothing to blunt the impact of a pair of wide, sky blue eyes. Her nose and chin were delicate, her cheeks softly contoured, the shape of her face a perfect heart. She wore a simple gray suit, which looked anything but drab on her.

His first thought as she placed her cup and saucer on the trolley and came around it to offer her hand, was that she'd better be genuine or he was going to be her first conquest.

Cordelia rose to introduce them. ''Kathy, this is our nephew, Gilbert London, who will protect you on the tour. Gib, darling, meet Kathy McQuade, your charge.''

Kathy took his hand in her firm, small one and

shook it. Her smile was warm and friendly—until she looked into his eyes and then he saw it flicker.

"Miss McQuade," he said politely.

Disappointment seemed to fill her gaze, and her hand tightened on his just a little—as though in challenge. But she, too, spoke politely. "Mr. London."

"Oh, come now, you two," Cordelia said. "Miss and Mr.? You're going to be tripping over each other for four weeks, confined in cars, in planes and hotel suites. I think the formalities can be dispensed with. Mrs. McQuade, our nephew, Gilbert. Gib, Kathy's mother, Patricia McQuade."

Gib was surprised to find the woman as beautiful as her daughter, with very little about her to betray her age. She had the same smile and the same firm handshake.

When she looked into Gib's eyes, her smile widened. Her eyes went speculatively up and down the length of him from head to toe, then across him from shoulder to shoulder. "You're a healthy specimen, Gib," she said with a nod that seemed to indicate approval. Gib heard Kathy's groan. "After Morganstern's show yesterday, I'm glad you'll be along. His challenge made me a little nervous."

"Gib was with Special Forces in Somalia," Rose said. "He knows what he's doing. You and Kathy will be safe."

"Shall we sit?" Cordelia suggested. "I have your itinerary, and though all the reservations are made, we can still make changes if there's anything you're not comfortable with."

Kathy looked over the ten-city schedule and found nothing to disapprove of. For someone who'd seldom left Bayside, Massachusetts, except for her five years at Boston College in Chestnut Hill, and the occasional trip to the Berkshires with friends, visiting ten big cities sounded like a luxury vacation.

She knew much of the time would be spent in tedious travel, and she was terrified by the thought of appearing on television, but otherwise she was as anxious for the tour as her mother was.

She hoped Gib London wasn't going to be a problem. She could see in his eyes that he'd already made the assumption that she was repressed and delusional. She'd grown accustomed to that from strangers, in the month since the *Bayside Bugle* had done a story about her and her book.

But she didn't like the thought of being confronted with that attitude on a daily basis when she would have to appear calm and confident before the media.

"Why don't we take your mother on a tour of our rose garden," Cordelia suggested, "so that you and Gib can get acquainted?"

Patsy stood immediately. "That would be lovely."

Gib got to his feet as the women trooped by him. Rose patted his arm. "Be nice, dear. She's important to us, so don't try to bully her like you bully us, all right?"

Lucinda took his other arm, coming to his defense. "Why, what a thing to say! He's never bullied us. He's always a complete gentleman."

Cordelia drew her sisters away. "He bullies us all the time, and very successfully," she said with a knowing glance at him over her shoulder. "So successfully that you two delicate flowers don't even notice. The only thing in his defense is that he's usually right.'' She paused in the doorway to wave at Kathy. ''We'll be back in a bit.''

The moment the ladies' voices dissolved toward the rear of the house, Kathy put her cup and saucer down and stood. She was generally not confrontational, but this trip had to be somewhat successful so that she could make a serious impression on her mother's debt.

She faced him, her stance a little rigid. They stood about three yards apart on the bright Oriental carpet. ''I would notice,'' she said.

He arched an eyebrow in question. ''Pardon me?''

''If you tried to bully me,'' she said directly, ''I would notice and probably not respond well. So if that's the way you usually operate, you might want to reconsider.''

He faced her squarely, his demeanor completely relaxed, hands in the pants pockets of a dark blue suit. Her mother had been right when she'd called him a healthy specimen. He was tall and big and apparently blessed with the confidence that came with size.

He was also very handsome in an angular sort of way—broad brow, strong nose, square jaw. His hair was golden brown and close-cropped, except for a little length right at the top where it lay in unruly charm from a side part. His eyes were hazel.

He noticed her careful study of him, but she met his gaze without flinching. They were supposed to get to know each other, after all.

''Are you suggesting I'd find it necessary to bully you?'' he asked.

''No,'' she replied. ''I'm saying that if you're the kind of man who has to get your way by bullying, we should know that now. And you should make other arrangements."

He seemed more amused than annoyed. "You're telling me you've taken an instant dislike to me?"

She struggled for patience. Things never went well when she tried to assert herself. She'd often wondered how her mother did it so easily. "No. Actually I think the reverse is true."

"Ah." He smiled. "An instant attraction, then?"

She came close to abandoning the struggle for patience, then remembered the need to practice poise for the tour. "No," she said again, breathless with the effort. "I meant that I noticed when we shook hands that you'd already dismissed me as anyone you would care to know."

That turned his smile to a look of puzzlement. "You misread me. I never make instant decisions about people."

She went past him to an embroidery stand, where a partially completed spray of white and pink roses had been worked into a square of claret velvet. She put a fingertip to a white rosebud done in a satin stitch. "Unless you're dealing with a mature woman who believes sex should mean something, then you can consider her crazy without having to know any more about her."

"I don't recall saying that."

She turned away from the stand with a resigned sigh. "You didn't have to. It was in your face. I get it all the time. Some people are downright antagonistic, and others are very polite, but I can see they think I'm suffering from some Freudian syndrome and they have to humor me."

He considered that, then suggested, "Maybe the

sudden public attention has made you a little defensive. But you must know that taking such a stand is going to draw challenges from all fronts.''

She nodded. ''I do.'' Then she stopped in the process of giving a standing globe a spin and offered a challenge of her own. ''I'm just not sure how much it will help me on this tour to be challenged from within my own camp. Of course, you're entitled to how you feel, but if we're going to be followed by reporters, photographers and cameramen, I think it would be detrimental if your scorn was visible to them.''

He took several steps toward her, a small flare of temper in his eyes. ''You know, if anything's going to count against you on this trip, it's your I-see-and-understand-everything attitude. I don't agree with your position, but it is a free country. And I remember what I was thinking when I shook your hand. It wasn't that you were crazy, but that you were very beautiful, and—'' he paused to grin ''—can you take this, Miss McQuade?''

She shifted impatiently. ''I'm a virgin, Mr. London, not a wimp. Do tell me.''

''All right.'' He took several more steps toward her. ''I was thinking that if the circumstances were different, *I* would be doing my best to make you change your mind.''

She remained absolutely still, not at all sure how to react to that statement. So she said the only thing she could think of to discourage him. ''I'm...seeing someone.''

Now the scorn in his eyes *was* clear. ''State Representative Neil Barton, now running for the United States Senate. He's made quite a point of your relationship. Probably makes him very popular with his conservative constituency."

Kathy felt herself bristle. "You're saying he has a motive for dating me?"

"I'm saying he has a motive for everything. And maybe we could find a way to get along if we stop trying to read each other's minds, all right? I don't care about your stand on sex, and I don't care about who you're seeing or why he's seeing you. All I'm concerned with is that my aunts get a good return on their investment in you."

Now she allowed herself to look scornful. "A good return for them also means a good return for you."

"A good return for them means they can eventually retire without having to sell their house."

She caught the globe with her elbow and set it rocking. "Well, I'm not sure we're going to get that with you on the tour."

He put a hand out to steady it. "Because I might try to compromise your principles?" he asked. "Or because you don't like the look in my eyes?"

"You couldn't compromise my principles," she assured him, heading for the shelter of her chair behind the tea trolley. "And you have quite nice eyes," she added boldly to show him she could hold her own, "but they might be too honest for something as revealing as a publicity tour."

"You're afraid the public will *see* that I find you sexy?"

She stopped behind the trolley to glare at him. "Grow up, London. You don't take me seriously. That's what I'm afraid they'll see."

He couldn't deny that she had a point. "All

right." He went to the chair opposite her, and when she sat, he did, too. "Then give me something I can take seriously."

Her blue eyes narrowed. "What do you mean?"

"Convince me that you're absolutely serious about this. That you're not taking my aunts and the public for a ride."

She studied him in disbelief for a moment, then she shook her head. "If I was going to 'take someone for a ride,' as you so originally put it, would I do it with a subject so unlikely to get popular support?"

"You really are a virgin?"

She rolled her eyes in exasperation. "I really am a virgin. Are you willing to take my word on that, or is there some kind of *test* you'd like to give me?"

He studied her with unsettling concentration, then he nodded finally. "I'll take you at your word, but understand that if you're proven wrong anywhere along the line, I'll make you pay back the company for every dime spent on you."

She got to her feet and went to him, hand held out. "That's a deal. But in all fairness, you have to promise not to say or do anything that'll suggest to the press that you don't believe in me."

That was only fair. He took her hand and shook it.

"Well, isn't that nice," Cordelia said, as the aunts and Patsy walked back into the room. Patsy was carrying an armload of roses wrapped in newspaper. "The children have made friends. That'll make everything so much easier."

Gib looked into Kathy's eyes and saw the same

grim amusement he felt. Nothing about this was going to be easy.

KATHY CHARGED UP her own Visa card with a vengeance. Her mother was thrilled as she added a soft blue sweater and skirt to a pile of other dresses and suits in soft colors and fabrics.

She bought shoes, jewelry, fragrances.

Kathy loaded everything into the car for the trip home, then stared guiltily at the array of purchases. They represented a good six or seven hundred dollars of her royalties that wouldn't go to pay off her mother's debts.

She couldn't explain what had possessed her when she'd looked into the mirror that morning after breakfast and had seen herself wearing a pair of brown slacks and a beige shirt. She'd looked plain, drab, lacking in sexual appeal. And she'd felt desperate, suddenly, to change that.

She wondered if it had been for herself or because she was about to embark on a four-week trip across the country with a man who'd said he found her sexy. A man who annoyed her certainly, and who represented an attitude she felt was responsible for the crumbling precipice on which many young people stood.

But she knew there were millions of young men out there just like him, who judged a woman on her appearance and who simply wouldn't take Kathy or her book seriously unless she at least looked like a woman they might find attractive.

"Why so gloomy?" her mother asked as she belted herself into the passenger seat.

Kathy put the key in the ignition of her silver

compact car. ''Buyer's remorse, I guess,'' she admitted.

Patsy swatted her knee. ''Don't be silly. You have to look wonderful to be thought wonderful. It isn't fair, but that's the way the world works. And it'll keep your bodyguard on his toes.''

Kathy turned the key, put the car in reverse and backed out of the parking space. ''Let's hope so,'' she said. ''I don't think he's on our side.''

Patsy laughed lightly. ''Well, of course he isn't. What man in his right mind would look at a beautiful woman and be happy with the news that she was a virgin and intended to remain so for the space of time they would spend together?''

Kathy braked at the stop sign where the parking lot met the street and blinked at her mother. ''Mom, that's archaic thinking. Why can't the man be as responsible for rational behavior in a relationship as the woman? Not that he and I have a relationship, but you know what I mean.''

''I do know what you mean, but you said it yourself in your book. Society raises itself to the level women demand. Many women today want to deny that responsibility—and they certainly can, I suppose, because maybe it isn't fair. But it's a truth nevertheless. Men are driven to populate the world. Part of a woman's job is to keep it a loving and peaceful place—whether you're Mrs. Fields or Madeleine Albright.''

Kathy turned onto the street with a groan. ''I wish,'' she said, ''that I'd written a book on gardening.''

GIB GLANCED over his itinerary as he stepped onto the elevator, then found himself shoved to the back as his aunts stepped on behind him. They all wore coats with antique broaches on the left shoulder and hats with fussy little feathers and veils.

A stranger getting onto the elevator now might think he'd passed through a time warp.

"Do you have your tickets?" Rose asked him. "And the company credit card?"

He patted his breast pocket. "Right here."

"I verified all your reservations," Lucinda said. "And you'll have a car and driver in every city."

"Thanks, Aunt Lucy."

"Publicity will be running two days ahead of you all along the way." Cordelia brushed lint off his shoulder. "Now, you will take good care of her, won't you? It isn't easy to stick your neck out and support an unpopular idea. Remember when you went on a hunger strike because your parents fired Mrs. Conrad?"

Now *he* felt as though he'd crossed through a time warp. He hadn't thought about Mrs. Conrad in twenty-five years. When he was a child, she'd been his parents' cook and housekeeper.

His mother and her second husband had fired her when Gib was nine because she'd grown old and slow and couldn't prepare the lower-in-fat *nouvelle cuisine* meals that would keep them presentable in their tennis shorts.

Gib had declared a hunger strike, promising that he wouldn't touch anything but water until she was reinstated. Nothing prepared by the young man hired to take her place could tempt Gib into eating—though he had to admit some of the food had great appeal.

But Mrs. Conrad had read to him, watched wrestling with him, interceded for him when he broke a neighbor's window with a killer Frisbee throw.

His aunts had visited and tried to sneak him food, but he'd refused on principle.

It jarred him to remember that.

When he'd fainted after four days, his mother rehired Mrs. Conrad.

"Aunt Cordie," he said, shaking off the memory, "don't worry. Nothing I do for you is ever half-hearted."

"I know, dear. But this is something you can do for yourself."

"I know. Whatever I do for the company ultimately benefits me."

His aunts shared a look, then Cordelia patted his arm. "Of course, Gilbert. But that's not what I meant. You're thirty-five."

He opened his mouth to tell her he knew how old he was, when Lucinda added gravely, "Don't you think it's time to think about a family? We're beginning to age, dear, and if you don't have children soon—"

"Beginning?" Rose interrupted with a musical laugh. "Darlings, let's face it. We're moldy figs."

Lucinda turned on her. "Rose, I wish you would not use that particular metaphor. It's one thing to use the term for problems that don't go away, but when you're referring to us I'd much prefer—" she thought a moment, then said grandly "—the last roses of summer."

The elevator doors had parted on the bottom floor of the office building, and a small group of custodial personnel stood just beyond the doors with buckets and boxes of cleaners, listening to the aunts argue.

Gib ushered them off the elevator and toward the large double doors while Rose and Lucinda continued to quarrel.

"We're worried about you, Gibby," Cordelia said as he opened the door for her. The other two aunts went through, still squabbling. Gib and Cordelia followed them toward the parking lot. "Your childhood was unusual, to say the least," Cordelia went on, "but you mustn't assume that all marriages are like the examples you've seen. Honestly. You went from parents who couldn't get along to all of those other relationships each of them had, still unable to find happiness. Then you played football in college, went to *war*—"

"It wasn't a war, it was—"

"A peacekeeping mission. I know. But you were shot at. And you've been involved in publishing ever since. If that isn't one skirmish after another, I don't know what is. Sometimes it seems that's what your whole life has been about. War."

"Aunt." Gib put an arm around her shoulders and squeezed gently. "That's why you've assigned me this particularly duty. I'm good at war."

Cordelia stopped. Lucinda and Rose continued on to the old Packard parked in a corner.

"I thought you would be good for Kathy," Cordelia said, looking into his eyes. "But I also thought Kathy would be good for you."

He wondered how to tell her virgins held no appeal for him, when she said briskly, "Oh, I know. You're a stud and you prefer a woman who's been around the block—preferably a couple of times."

He bit back the smile before it could form.

"But I'm telling you," she went on, "that love is stronger than war, so if you're intending to continue on this lonely rogue path you've set upon, you'd better watch yourself here."

He shook his head. "Auntie, she's into holding on to her love. So there's no danger."

His aunt smiled with a wickedness he usually only saw over contract negotiations. "Not so. She's saving it—for the right man."

"That isn't me."

She patted his cheek, then kissed it. "I guess we'll see if you're still feeling that way when you fly home from Los Angeles in four weeks."

"Aunt..."

"I know. I'm a pain in the posterior. So my sisters are always telling me."

Gib walked Cordelia to the Packard, hugged Lucinda and Rose, listened to all their cautions one more time, then waved them off as the old car chugged out of the parking lot and Cordelia plunged aggressively into traffic with a blare of her horn.

As he considered himself, embarking on this tour with Kathy McQuade and her mother, he thought that he seemed a lot like the Packard, being driven into traffic with some daredevil at the wheel.

Only he didn't even have a horn.

GIB PICKED UP the McQuade ladies the following morning at their home in Bayside, about twenty miles north of Boston. They had six bags between them and insisted on helping him carry them down the apartment's narrow stairs.

"Why don't you wait for me up here," he suggested, a bag in each hand and one under his right arm, "do a last-minute check to make sure you haven't left the iron on or something, and I'll get the bags down."

Kathy smiled pleasantly, holding the handle of a suit bag with two hands. "No," she said. "I'll be right behind you. And you should probably put one of those bags down. The stairway's very narrow."

It was a good thing he'd decided not to let her annoy him, he thought, as he ignored her suggestion and started down the stairs. Otherwise she'd already be doing it, and this was only the first hour of a month-long association that was bound to make him crazy.

Fortunately craziness was the prevailing approach to business at London Publishing.

She'd been right about the stairway. Three steps down, he'd already scraped the knuckles of his right hand against the rough wall and had to turn sideways.

Kathy followed patiently behind him, one step at a time, and though she said nothing, he was sure she was enjoying his laborious crablike descent.

"Shall I get the door?" she asked when they'd reached the bottom. "Or is it bodyguard policy for you to go through it first?"

He stood in the narrow space between the bottom of the stairs and the door to the outside and turned to look at her over his shoulder. The space was so small that she still stood on the last step. "You're haranguing me and we haven't even officially started the tour."

Her smile widened. "You consider that a harangue? Wait till you've spent some time with my mother. She makes me look like a silent movie."

"*Can* you get the door?" he asked. There wasn't room for her to move around him.

"Sure." She put her case down on the stair, leaned around him on the side that held just one bag, turned the knob and pushed the door open. Then she stood on tiptoe to hold it open as he pushed his way through.

On the other side of it, he held it open for her with his foot. She hurried through, her case half-dragged, half-carried in two hands.

He led the way to his Lexus, ignoring the warm spot on the outside of his arm where her breast had squashed against him when she reached for the door. No big deal. He had a sports jacket on and she wore a thick sweater. They'd made nothing near contact, so why did he feel as though he'd been tattooed there?

Some long-suppressed virgin fantasy from his adolescence, he guessed.

Ridiculous, really, when he considered he could make a phone call this afternoon and spend the night in the company of any of a number of women who would generously offer all to him.

"I don't understand why we're spending two nights in a Boston hotel," Kathy said, pausing to catch her breath, "when I live only twenty miles away. Mom and I could easily drive back home and save London Publishing several hundred dollars."

Gib unlocked the trunk and loaded her bags into it. "No. The aunts thought it was important that we give you star-quality treatment from the outset so that everyone's entirely convinced of our confidence in the book."

She grunted as she lifted her bag. He took it from her and placed it beside the other in the trunk of his car.

"Everyone's confidence but yours," she said, stepping back as he closed the trunk.

He glanced at her, locking it again. "You don't sound like a silent movie to me."

"How many women have you been with?" she asked abruptly.

He pocketed his keys. It was a sunny and beautiful day in early October, oaks and maples on the side street a riot of color against a clear blue sky.

Had he gone to work for Browning Books, he speculated, he could probably have fit in a round of golf this afternoon.

"Not a polite question," he said, heading off toward the apartment house at a swift pace.

She had to run to keep up with him. "No, I think you're wrong," she said. "Because the dating scene has forced a change in the code of courtesy. If you had asked me out, that's the first question I'd ask you."

He kept walking. "Okay, but I haven't asked you out, and if I had, your question would have precluded a second date and any hope of intimacy between us."

"That's my point exactly."

He didn't want to encourage her, but she'd lost him completely and he had to stop just short of the door and frown down at her. "How, exactly?"

"We date to select a life partner."

He shifted his weight impatiently. "We date to

make friends. To get to know people. To find someone with a common interest..."

She was nodding before he'd finished. "I know. That's ideally how it's supposed to be. That may even be how it starts, but the instant interest is engaged, that changes. We lead with our emotions, and if I haven't asked you the right questions at the outset, I'll find myself in your arms some starry night and wondering the morning after if I'd contracted something painful or messy or even fatal. Or if I'm pregnant."

He put his hands in his pockets. She looked so earnest, the sunlight making a ruby of her hair, that he forced himself to reply reasonably. "There are protections against those things easily available for a very reasonable price."

"Do you have one in your pocket right now?"

"Are you propositioning me?"

"If I did, would you have protection?"

He hated to have to admit it to her, because he knew where she was going with this. "No, I don't." He reached the door in two strides, pulled it open and indicated with a sweep of his arm that she should precede him. "I'm spending the next month with *you*, after all," he reminded her. "I didn't think it would be necessary. And you're seeing someone, remember?"

She went inside and waited for him on the bottom stair. "Good point," she said. "If we hadn't asked some pertinent questions first, you wouldn't know that about me, and you might find yourself all entangled and then discover that I present a threat to your emotional well-being. There are sexually transmitted disappointments as well as diseases, you know."

"And no condom to protect you from that."

The stairway was too narrow to allow them to go up side by side, so he put a hand to her back to encourage her to start climbing. He followed a step below her.

"I was trying to say," she finished as they ran up the stairs, "that it's easier to be celibate than to count on always being protected."

"On what planet? Making love is an important means of communication."

"Oh, please. That's the kind of attitude that's helped us raise much of a generation that discounts intelligence and conversation as a way of getting to know someone."

They reached the doorway to her apartment as he caught her arm to prevent her from going in. "How many men have you been with," he asked, "who've done more than provide intelligent conversation?"

"I've been kissed," she replied a little defensively.

"In a way that's made you want to stop intelligent conversation and just feel?"

Her eyes seemed to scan the air between them and he knew she was thinking. "Once or twice," she replied finally.

"And that never made you feel as though you were missing anything?"

She smiled ruefully at him. "Only those things we just talked about that you aren't carrying protection against." She pushed the door open, picked up one of the other two bags at the edge of the living room and started down again.

Lord, he thought, picking up the last bag. *This is going to be a long month.*

Chapter Three

Patsy was already in the limo Cordelia had hired to get Kathy and her mother and Gib to the television station, but Kathy was still behind the locked bathroom door in their suite at the Boston Park Plaza Hotel.

Gib paced nervously. She was scheduled to appear on a live call-in TV show at 8:00 p.m., and it was 7:31, barely enough time for the makeup woman to powder Kathy's nose before she went on the air.

"Kathy!" he called through the door. "We have to leave now or you're going to be on the nightly news as a no-show on 'Nighttime Boston'!"

The door opened and she stood there in a simple black dress made stunning by her red hair. She'd tamed it somewhat for the appearance by tucking it back on one side with a tortoiseshell comb.

Her face, though, was paper white, her eyes beautifully made up but huge.

He took her arms, certain she was about to dissolve. "What?" he asked anxiously.

"Nothing serious," she said breathlessly, her arms trembling under his hands. "Unless terror is serious. Is it? I mean, you've done this before? People get over it? Or...used to it?''

He'd have poured her a brandy, but there wasn't time. He snatched her wrap, a small jacket that matched her dress, off a nearby chair and put it around her shoulders and led her toward the door.

''I haven't done this before,'' he said honestly, ''but you know your subject so well, you'll relax the moment you start answering questions. I know it's scary, but it's just local television. It doesn't get the millions you get on national broadcasts.''

''Really? Like how many?''

''Couple of hundred thousand.''

He got her out the door and into the hallway, but she stopped on the way to the elevators. ''People?'' she asked in frightened disbelief.

He had to get tough here. He put his hands on her shoulders. ''People, Kathy. That's what we want. Think what it'll do for your sales if you get even half of them interested in what you have to say.''

She thought about that, then drew a breath and refocused on his face with a wan little smile. ''Want to go for a burger instead?''

''You get through this,'' he bargained, ''and I'll take you and your mom anywhere you want to go.''

She drew another breath, but she was still shaking. She tucked her arm in his as he led her to the elevator, and he got the feeling that at that moment he was essential to her survival.

She kept a grip on him in the back of the limo and didn't let go until they reached the television station and were greeted by the producer, who was beside herself with relief.

Neil Barton was waiting in the lobby, and Gib was abandoned as Kathy flew into Barton's arms.

"What are you doing here?" she demanded excitedly, color returning to her face.

Barton wrapped an arm around her shoulders and followed the producer into the elevator. Gib caught Patsy's arm as they hurried to get onto the car.

Barton greeted Patsy politely, and she responded in kind, then rolled her eyes at Gib the moment Barton turned back to Kathy.

Waiting in the green room with Patsy, Gib did his best to maintain a professional outlook, to assess the impression Kathy made and try to note what she could improve upon or change.

But he had a little difficulty doing that. He could still remember her clutching his arm as though he was all that stood between her and her fears.

But then she'd run into Barton's arms the moment he appeared, so Gib didn't see why he had to feel empathetic. If she was afraid, she'd get over it. If she wanted to sell books, she would, and that was why they were here, after all.

"She looks wonderful," Patsy said, sitting on the edge of a chair she'd pulled up to the small monitor. She turned to Gib for confirmation. "Doesn't she? I mean, she's a little nervous, but she looks wonderful."

She did. Her beautiful pink-and-ivory color was back, and she was eloquent, if a little stiff.

Then the interviewer invited Barton before the camera for a few moments just before the station break, explaining to the audience that Barton had taken up Kathy's cause and had stopped by to lend support. The rumor, he said, was that they were seeing each other. Was that true?

Kathy relaxed a little when Barton sat on the sofa beside her, but she did try to deflect the question. Barton, however, took advantage of it. ''We've dated three or four times,'' he said with a glance at Kathy that caressed her, but with the careful respect one would accord a virginal woman.

Patsy muttered an expletive at the television.

''I can't work hard for the Commonwealth of Massachusetts,'' Barton went on, ''and allow myself to be distracted by such a brilliant and beautiful young woman. I'm waging a valiant struggle, but I think I'm losing.''

That look again on his face.

That expletive again from Patsy's lips.

The interviewer turned to his viewing audience with a suggestive grin. ''Is there a threat to Miss McQuade's stand from our very own Representative Barton, candidate for the senate? Join us when we come back.''

Patsy stood up, as though she'd been ejected from her chair. ''I hope you're carrying a gun,'' she said to Gib as she went to a table that held fruit and crackers and other things to nibble on. ''If that man proposes to my daughter, I want you to kill him. Carrot stick? Cheese ball?''

''No, thanks.'' Gib went to the window that looked out over the lights of Boston—church spires, historic sites, government and commercial buildings all trying to claim his attention. But he was too annoyed with Barton.

He understood Patsy's dislike of the man. She was

a very direct woman, and Barton was a politician through and through.

Some men made honorable contributions to the states and the country they represented by playing the games politics had so refined. Deals, bargains, one principle sometimes sacrificed in the interest of another that resulted, hopefully, in the common good.

But he didn't think that was what Barton was about. Despite his tall good looks, there was something in his face Gib didn't trust. He wasn't sure what it was, but he trusted his own instincts.

And though Gib had been a bodyguard only four hours, he had the uneasy feeling that Barton represented a danger to Kathy.

"I don't believe for a minute that his feelings are sincere," Patsy said, taking a plateful of snacks back to her chair in front of the monitor. "Last year he was dating Susan Waldman, the socialite who was working to protect the wetlands. I think he just takes up with whoever has the public's attention and can get him what *he* wants."

"Nighttime Boston" was on the air again, and Kathy and Barton were laughing in the background, heads close together, as the host announced their return.

"She seems to like him," Gib observed.

"That's because she has no long-term experience with men," Patsy said, pointing a cracker at the monitor. "Her father died when she was nine, and I was too busy keeping the print shop going to date. She went to an all-women's college, and manages a bookstore to support her writing habit. She's only twenty-six. She's smart and somewhat savvy, but pretty much an innocent where men are concerned. There just haven't been any in her life.''

''How did she meet Barton?''

''She volunteers at Loaves and Fishes on Fridays, and Barton was on a campaign tour and worked in the kitchen for a couple of hours. I think she likes him because it's nice to have an ally—especially a somewhat powerful one.''

''You don't think her heart's involved?''

He thought he'd asked that easily enough, but Patsy turned away from the monitor to smile at him. ''No, I don't. He's taken her to a fund-raising dinner and a couple of other political events—just to show her off, I think. Why?''

He looked away from her speculative gaze to study the screen. ''I'm just wondering how upset she'll get when I keep him at a distance tonight.''

''Mmm,'' she replied, interest ripe in her voice. ''So am I.''

Kathy took only one hostile call toward the end of the program. Until then the callers were mostly older women, clergy and anxious parents who praised her stand. Then James from Gloucester called.

''Get real, Miss McQuade,'' he said. He sounded young, Gib thought. Maybe college age. ''Do you really want young people, who have nothing in this world but each other, to give up even that?''

Barton frowned, but Kathy moved closer to her microphone. ''No, of course not,'' she replied. ''But I think young people would have the potential for a much brighter future if they come together in mind and spirit before they come together in bed.''

''I'm a struggling student from a low-income family,'' he countered. ''I got here on a scholarship, but I don't have a dime to spend on movies or theater tickets or eating out. My girlfriend's poor, too. We can't afford to go anywhere, so we just come back here to this place I share with three other guys. The rule is if the shade on the front door is down, you don't come home until it's up again.''

The host smiled at the camera with a knowing nod, suggesting he remembered a similar code from his own youth.

Then the camera closed in on Kathy and caught the concentration in her eyes. ''I can sympathize with your circumstances, James. It's hard to be broke. But, in my opinion, if you and your girlfriend feel as though you share something valuable, you should mean more to each other than free entertainment.''

''Well—'' James paused ''—we're not planning to get married, or anything. We're just enjoying the moment.''

''Then you *are* just free entertainment for each other?''

''Yeah. What's wrong with that?''

''Could you substitute any other young woman for your girlfriend and be as happy with the result?''

James paused again and Gib couldn't help but wonder if James was staring down the business end of his girlfriend's broom. ''Ah...no.''

''Then she's something special.''

''Yes.''

''That you're treating like free entertainment?''

There was another pause, then the line went dead.

Kathy leaned back in her chair. ''My point is,'' she said to the audience, ''that James and his girlfriend probably got together because they cared about each other, but their relationship got physical before they had time to discover anything else about each other.

"If you're out there, young and broke, Boston offers scores of things to do that don't cost a dime. Explore each other's minds while you're exploring Boston. There'll be plenty of time later for love-making."

"All right! That's all we have time for." The host thanked Kathy for her appearance, and Barton for stopping by and adding substance to the rumor that they were becoming an item.

Barton squeezed Kathy's shoulders and smiled into her clearly relieved face as the credits rolled and a voice-over announced that the nine o'clock news would follow.

"WELL." Patsy rose, her plate empty. "Except for that little weasel, I'd say she was successful. What do you think, Gib?"

He nodded. "She's good. I think it was a fine start."

"Autograph party tomorrow afternoon, then we're off to New York?"

"Right. Come on. We have to decide where to go for dinner."

Kathy was coming into the green room just as Gib opened the door. Patsy flew into her arms. "You were wonderful!" she praised. "Gib thinks it was a good start."

"Good." Kathy was a little flushed, now that it was over. She put a hand to her heart and closed her eyes. "I am so relieved that it went well."

Patsy laughed. "Of course, James from Gloucester's girlfriend is probably pummeling him right now."

Kathy made a face. "I wish he hadn't hung up."

Barton caught Kathy's arm. "I'm taking Kathy to dinner. I'll have her back—"

"No." Gib spoke quietly but clearly. "We're going to dinner together, but you're welcome to join us."

"Look—" Barton began to protest.

Gib cut him off. "My job is to stay with her. Would you like to join us?"

"London, I am a representative elected by the people of the Commonwealth of Massachusetts." Barton bristled indignantly, and his chest seemed to swell with the effort to convey his importance. "I can be trusted to keep Kathy safe."

"Maybe." Gib looked him over, unable to convince himself that that was true. He was sure that showed in his eyes. "But who's going to protect her from you?"

Kathy and Barton both sputtered indignantly.

Gib pointed to the monitor behind him. "You just told half a million people how much you care for her. Come on, Barton. We're both men of the world. The way she looked and presented herself tonight, you want me to believe you don't have lust in your heart?"

It was a trap, and Gib sprang it without conscience. If Barton admitted that he did, then Gib had won. If he said he didn't, it might offend Kathy and make Barton look like less than the attentive man he claimed to be.

Barton made a last stand. "Fine," he said stiffly.

"Then we'll meet you at the Fox and Hound back at your hotel."

"I'm sorry," Gib said. "I've made reservations at the Polonaise. You can meet us there. Kathy is riding with her mother and me."

Barton's eyes promised retribution.

Gib ignored him as he picked up the jacket Kathy had left on a chair before going on camera. When he went to help Kathy into it, Barton was gone.

"That was a transparent bit of muscle flexing," Kathy said, temper bright in her eyes. "And completely unnecessary."

They went out into the hall, and Gib closed the door behind them. "I don't agree. My aunts are expecting me to do my job."

"That should include exercising some control over personal prejudices." That line delivered, Kathy set off down the hall, the heels of her shoes reverberating loudly.

Patsy elbowed Gib in the ribs. "Good work," she praised quietly, then hurried after her daughter.

BARTON DIDN'T MEET them for dinner. Kathy got a message from the maître d' saying that Barton had been beeped on his way to the restaurant but would come to the hotel tomorrow night to say goodbye, since he wouldn't see her for four weeks.

Annoyed because Gib had spoiled her happiness over her first successful interview, Kathy cast him a grim glance as she folded the note and tucked it into her purse.

"I hope you're happy," she said. "He isn't coming. He'll stop by the hotel to say goodbye tomorrow night."

"What *urgent business* called him away?" Gib didn't even pretend disappointment at Neil's absence. And his emphasis on the words *urgent business* suggested that he didn't believe it was that at all that kept him away.

"He probably doesn't want to get indigestion from eating with *you.*" She brutally stabbed her fork into the restaurant's signature veal in gooseberry sauce.

"Really." He met her angry gaze without flinching. "Well, if I were him and I claimed to be losing the battle to not get involved with you, I wouldn't let me discourage me."

"Yeah, well, we're not all combat trained, you know."

"Oh, I bet infighting goes on among politicians that would curl a soldier's hair."

That remark sent her eyes to his hair, where she was momentarily distracted by the blond-brown strands that lay in attractive rebellion across his brow. She guessed it would be springy to the touch.

Then she remembered that he'd just ruined her evening and turned to her mother for conversation.

GIB *WAS* AN ASSET at Kathy's autograph party the following day, though, when picketers for free love tried to enter the Cambridge bookstore. He kept them outside.

"Free love," her mother said when the bookstore owner brought them into the back room for a cup of coffee and a pastry after three hours of signing. The line of eager readers who awaited Kathy's autograph was still at least an hour long. "That's a group from

Victorian days that sort of got resurrected in the sixties."

Kathy sipped her coffee gratefully. "I guess some people think restrictions of any kind are detrimental to us."

"You do understand that Gib wasn't just being arbitrary last night." Her mother offered her a bite-size éclair. "I hope they're not going to feed us like this everywhere we go. We'll have to get new wardrobes by New Orleans."

"He *was* being arbitrary," Kathy insisted, only a little distracted by the delicious éclair. She chewed and swallowed, then wiped her fingers on a napkin. "He doesn't like Neil because Neil believes as I do—that sex can wait. I'm sure Gib thinks Neil less of a man because of it, and that's why he likes to bait him. And Neil won't respond because of me."

"Maybe he can't respect Neil because he knows Neil is using you."

Kathy crushed her napkin in her fist and pointed a finger at her mother. "No, *you* think Neil is using me. Which really makes no sense at all when you think about it, because Jack Trent *did* use you, and yet you won't file charges against him. Explain that to me."

"I can't."

"Then leave Neil alone."

"Jack," Patsy said after a long sip of coffee, "was a good man who sometimes can't help himself. Neil is a stupid man who tries to look good while doing bad things and thinks no one will notice. Of course there's you, who *doesn't* notice."

"That is so unfair I won't even comment on it."

Kathy popped another éclair into her mouth, chewed and swallowed, then freshened her makeup.

"Gib, on the other hand," Patsy went on, "is a good man who seems determined to keep his promises."

"Mom, forgive me, but you're not the best judge of character."

"Cordelia told me he was decorated for conspicuous bravery in Somalia for defending civilians threatened by those paramilitary hoodlums. There was a bounty on his head after that."

Kathy listened in sober surprise, then ran a brush quickly through her hair and forced herself to dispel an image of Gib London dressed in camouflage and staring down an enemy.

"Well," she said, turning toward the door to the shop, "someone should tell him that you can't use the same tactics in everyday life that you use on the battlefield."

"I wish you could," Patsy whispered after her as she followed her to the table. "I'd use a bazooka on you!"

"I don't think they use bazookas anymore."

"Well, I'd find one in a war surplus store."

"WE SOLD 237 books today!" the joyous bookseller reported to Kathy that evening in a telephone call to the hotel. After the long day in the bookstore, Kathy and her mother opted for room service and an evening in their robes. They sat at the table eating Caesar salads.

Gib, in old cords and an MIT sweatshirt, sat in a corner of the suite's living room on his cellular phone, a hand covering his free ear, verifying the following day's travel arrangements.

"That's wonderful, Mr. Waldport," Kathy replied. "I had visions of you having to return most of them for credit."

"Nope," Waldport replied. "We made a killing. Tell Gib that one of the free-love ladies left him her phone number. Ready to take it down?"

Kathy jotted the number on an unused napkin.

"Her name is Clementine Shaw."

"Got it."

"Thanks, Kathy. You want to show up for a signing on your way back, give me two days' warning and I'll get the books in. I'll bet we could sell as many all over again."

"Thanks, Mr. Waldport."

When Kathy hung up the phone, she told her mother about the number of books sold.

Patsy called the figure across the room to Gib, who was just lowering the antenna on his cell phone. He came to the table with a smile and sat in the third place where a cup of coffee stood next to a Reuben sandwich.

"Good work," he said. "I had my hands full keeping you safe from a group that was convinced you were held in virgin enslavement by London Publishing."

Kathy smiled sweetly and handed him the napkin on which she'd taken the note. "Apparently one of the women your hands were filled with would like to see you again—name of Clementine."

He frowned over the note, then put it aside and grinned at Patsy. "Clementine. She wants to free me from the bondage of my employment by showing me how to make love while windsurfing."

"Oooh." Patsy's eyes lost focus as she appeared to concentrate on the thought. "That does have a certain appeal. Two bodies being tossed around by a honey-scented wind determined to let nature take them where she wills."

Gib picked up a sandwich half, smiling at her in surprise. "I didn't think so. I like my comfort. A feather bed—on a blanket in front of a fire—in a hot tub."

Patsy sighed wistfully. "Yeah. Those, too."

Kathy looked from her mother to Gib, who also seemed lost in thought, and felt that little niggle of resentment she always experienced when people talked about sex, or laughed knowingly over jokes.

At this point, she knew as much about sex as an inexperienced adolescent. Well, she might know more about it, but none of that knowledge had come from direct experience. It came from what she'd garnered from other people's conversations, from books and movies.

Kissing was nice, though not all that remarkable. And she'd warded off all intimate touch because she wanted to save that, too, for someone she loved and who loved her.

So she'd never been to that place that transcended the here and now, that made the kind of memories that induced the distant stares her mother and Gib now wore.

She couldn't help but wonder what the woman had been like who'd inspired that look in Gib. A passionate brunette? A cool blonde?

Conversation resumed, but Kathy remained quiet.

Gib and her mother talked about tomorrow's flight to New York and Kathy's various appearances, while Kathy wondered how this had all happened to her in the first place.

She hadn't set out to be a virgin. Though comfortable on her own, she'd wanted to find a strong, fun-loving man who wanted children and a life of passion and adventure. Her own childhood had been rather quiet because her mother worked long hours to meet deadlines. Kathy had often longed for siblings and noisy activity. But she hadn't found that man in college, nor in the bookstore where she'd worked since then. And he certainly wasn't to be found in her apartment building filled with little old ladies and married couples. She felt as though her life hung suspended, waiting.

But she knew he was out there, somewhere. She knew it with a certainty that was startling in its power. And that was how it had become easy to store up all her dreams for him, to save all the love that bloomed in her and label it his.

The only thing that worried her was that life had a sense of humor. She could imagine it laughing as it maneuvered them around within the tracks of their lives so that they passed closely but never touched, missing each other time after time until they were too sensible for passion, too old for adventure.

And then she would have missed everything.

But she couldn't think that way. She was still very young, with her whole life ahead of her, and there was no sense in borrowing trouble.

She didn't know if Neil Barton was him or not. He was attentive and there was something in his eyes when he looked at her, but his presence didn't relieve her of the sense of waiting.

She could be wrong about that, she supposed. Maybe whatever life gave you, you found yourself waiting for something more, something else. And right now Neil was a good man to have on her side. Her mother suggested that Neil was using her, and though Kathy didn't believe it, she guessed that was only fair because in a way she was using his support.

Room service had cleared away their dinners, and Kathy was repacking when Gib rapped on her bedroom door to tell her Neil had arrived. Her mother had gone down to the lounge to meet a friend who'd once worked with her and now lived in Boston.

Kathy pulled on a pair of dark jade sweats and went out into the living room to meet Neil. Gib went into the small kitchen that was separated from the living room by a breakfast counter.

Neil pulled Kathy down beside him on the sofa, which was upholstered in ivory brocade. He looked stricken and depressed. "Four weeks is going to seem like an eternity," he said, putting an arm around her and drawing her close. "You have to call me once a day and tell me how you're doing."

Kathy snuggled closer, warmed by his concern and the genuine distress in his eyes. "I've got your cell phone number, and you have Gib's."

Neil rolled his eyes. "Don't let him browbeat you."

"He hasn't tried."

"I'm sure he will. I think sending him with you was a bad idea."

"I'll be fine. Don't worry about it. Just concentrate on your campaign." Kathy glanced toward the kitchen where Gib seemed to be taking his time making a fresh pot of coffee. She wondered if he was doing it deliberately so that he could eavesdrop on their conversation. After his behavior the night before, when Neil had wanted to drive her to the restaurant, she wouldn't put it past him.

Despite her assurances to Neil, she knew Gib was going to be trouble on this trip. But she didn't want to think about that now.

"Have they finished framing your house yet?" she asked, trying to distract Neil as his eyes, too, wandered toward the kitchen. He was building a traditional Cape Cod in Rockport. "Just this morning," he replied, a smile wiping away the concern in his face. "When you come back, you can help me pick out appliances and carpet and all that stuff."

"That'll be fun."

"If all goes according to plan, we should be able to celebrate Christmas at my place."

"Aren't you going to Hyannis to be with your family?"

"They're going to London to be with my grandmother." He leaned forward to look gravely into her eyes. "This Christmas is just going to be you and me." And then he kissed her—or tried to.

"Pardon me," a deep voice interrupted.

Kathy, one hand pushing against Neil's chest, turned to see Gib sitting on the edge of the coffee table in front of the sofa. He was close enough that she could see the cool determination in his hazel eyes.

"What?" she demanded.

"Just doing my job." He looked from Kathy to

Neil with an apologetic smile she didn't believe for a moment. "It's time for Neil to leave."

Neil stood as though he were on a spring, and pointed a finger down at Gib's face. "Look, you!" He spoke in a barely controlled voice, face flushed, eyes blazing. "No one throws me out of anywhere! I came to say goodbye to Kathy, and that's what I'm going to do!"

Gib got to his feet with easy movements that contrasted sharply with Neil's display of temper. "That's fine," he said. "Just do it without the hands and the tongue."

Neil grabbed Gib's chambray shirtfront in his fist. He was as tall as Gib and similarly built, but had none of the muscle tone visible in the other man's movements.

And the fact that Gib didn't move a muscle filled the moment with tension and a score of dangerous possibilities.

Kathy leaped to her feet and tried to get between them.

Gib caught her arm in steely fingers and pushed her out of the way. "I don't want you nearby," he said without moving his eyes from Neil, "when he goes flying."

Neil made a scornful sound, but Kathy noticed that the fist holding a clump of Gib's shirt clenched and unclenched nervously. "You and what army?" Neil asked.

Kathy groaned. "Please. This is so high school!" She tried to intervene again, but Gib pushed her gently away.

"You have five seconds to get your hand off me," he said to Neil, his tone almost amiable, "or you're not going to own it anymore. And the rest of you is going to go sailing off that balcony and over downtown Boston.''

The men stared at each other.

Knowing Neil needed an excuse to help him save face, Kathy gave it to him. ''Neil, please,'' she said. ''For me.''

Neil dropped his hand, though it still twitched nervously. ''I'm doing it for her,'' he said belligerently. ''When the tour is over, London, you and I are going to have it out.''

''Better buff up on your follow-through before then,'' Gib replied as Neil went to the door.

Neil stopped as though he would have turned back, but Kathy caught his arm and walked him to the door. ''I appreciate your coming by. And I'll call you whenever I get the chance.''

Neil tore his angry glance from Gib, who watched them from the middle of the room, and smiled into Kathy's upturned face. ''I'm not walking away from him again,'' he promised grimly. ''Don't ask me to.''

In defiance of Gib, Kathy reached up to kiss Neil's cheek. ''I'll see you in four weeks. Think cheerful thoughts. Nobody wants a sour-faced senator.''

Neil stepped out into the hall. He finally smiled. ''You'd better miss me,'' he ordered.

''I will.'' She pulled the door partially closed, thinking that if Neil wanted to take advantage of the moment, he could.

But he didn't. He blew her a kiss, then turned in the direction of the elevators.

Kathy closed the door and marched to the middle

of the room where Gib still stood. "If we're going to survive together on this tour," she said, her voice quietly angry, "we're going to have to get a few things straight."

He nodded. "You behave unfavorably to being told what to do. We've already covered that."

She looked at him in disbelief. "Then why did you do it?"

He returned the look. "Did you think the possibility of your anger would prevent me from doing my job? And I didn't tell you what to do, anyway. I told *him*."

"I was involved in the kiss, too. When you stopped him, you stopped *me*."

"You're a virgin, remember?"

"I'm a virgin!" She spread her arms in exasperation. "Not a frigid prude. I wanted that kiss!"

He studied her bristling demeanor with interest, then said calmly, "Well, if all you want is a kiss, I'll give you one."

She was rendered speechless by the suggestion, but only momentarily. Anger swelled in her, but right beside it was a traitorous burst of excitement. She tried to ignore it.

"I wanted *Neil's* kiss," she said disdainfully.

He looked heavenward in supplication. "You can't be serious. You gave him two chances to tell me to go to hell—once when you kissed him at the door, and then when you tried to hide behind the half-closed door. But he didn't, did he?"

He hadn't. She was trying to dismiss a slight disappointment over that by telling herself that he'd simply used common sense.

She turned the conversation in another direction.

"Why would *you* want to kiss me? You told me you don't like virgins."

"I don't have to like it," he replied, unfolding his arms. "You're the one who wants it."

Kathy was distracted by the seeds of a familiar argument often offered by her opposition. "So sex and the little rituals that lead up to it don't have to mean anything?"

Gib shifted his weight and put his hands in his pockets. "At the risk of offending your virginal sensibilities, I don't think they do. You attach more importance to them than they deserve. They're a natural function intended to bring pleasure and comfort. That's all."

She had to give him credit for at least sounding regretful of his opinion. "Then you think you could make me like your kisses even without your emotional involvement in them."

He inclined his head. She interpreted the gesture as a concession to modesty. "My skill would be involved," he said. "And my wholehearted interest in the exercise, of course."

She was more fascinated than repelled by his arrogance. "Skill," she repeated.

An openhanded gesture, this time, to express modesty. "I'm only repeating what the ladies have told me."

"The legions that I was rude enough to ask about the other day?"

"Yes."

Kathy sighed as she made a production of considering the suggestion. "To a woman who is very selective about who she kisses, I think I want to be assured of more than skill. A skilled painting without heart is just a painting. Only the soul of the artist can make it a masterpiece."

He challenged her with a smile. "You ask a lot of just a kiss."

"See, that's the point," she said. "It should never be 'just a kiss.' And if we didn't offer them to all and sundry, but to those for whom we feel something, they *would* be special. We *would* have masterpieces."

The challenge remained in place. "Then you *don't* want the kiss?"

He was giving the little virgin a graceful out, just as she'd helped Neil save face a few moments ago. But she liked to think she didn't need a break.

"I didn't say that." She took a step toward him and saw the surprise in the depths of his eyes.

When he didn't move to take her into his arms, to assume control, she felt momentarily at a loss. She tried to turn that to her advantage. "You don't mind my being in charge?"

He took a step toward her. That left a hair's breadth between them. "No one's in charge," he corrected. "It's a mutual communication. Although you and your masterpiece theory have put a little more pressure on me than I'm used to."

"Do you want to change your mind?" She almost hoped he'd say yes.

But he said no, firmly. Then he asked, "You?"

Her no was a little faint. Then she remembered that she was trying to make a point here, just as he was.

She looped her arms around his neck.

His hands come up gently to her shoulderblades. She felt the warmth in them through her sweatshirt, the strength in them gentled. It was hard to believe these were the same hands that had moved her out of the way when Neil had grabbed him.

She lifted her mouth toward him and watched, her heart thudding, as he lowered his head to meet her lips.

Chapter Four

Gib covered her mouth with his in complete confidence. He'd kissed scores of women in varying degrees of passion in as many different romantic venues. It was always nice.

He hadn't kissed a virgin since high school, however, and as much as he found Kathy McQuade interesting in other areas, he expected this encounter to be dull.

He was wrong.

The first thing he noticed was that her movement into his arms was not at all tentative. That set him slightly off balance immediately. He couldn't decide whether to be flattered or offended that she wasn't even a little nervous.

After two seconds, however, he no longer cared because other things claimed his attention.

Her lips were warm and met his with a readiness that sharpened his awareness a notch. Then he noticed her hands at the back of his neck, her fingertips moving into his hair, both hands cupping the back of his head as he leaned over her, newly dedicated to the experience.

He opened his mouth over hers, expecting her to

withdraw. But she parted her lips, her tongue meeting the tip of his, and they battled slowly—a tender advance and retreat, give and take.

Then he became aware that all of her was pressed to all of him. He wondered absently what she was doing, then realized it wasn't *her* doing at all, but his. He had one arm around her torso and the other around her waist and he was crushing her to him.

Then one of her fingers was tracing the rim of his ear and her lips were at his other ear, her breath sighing into it as she kissed him there.

He felt as though she'd punched him instead of kissed him. His ears were ringing, his mouth was numb, his body ached as though he'd been pummeled.

He knew a moment close to panic.

One of the advantages to a casual approach to sex was the ability to remain just a little above the passion, to be able to monitor the situation, gauge performance, then adjust it according to the data collected.

But when he tried to do those things, he didn't seem able to maintain the neutrality required. He seemed to be all beating heart and raw nerve endings.

It occurred to him that while Kathy's fragile frame felt very small in his arms, her presence seemed suddenly too big for the moment, too large for his space.

He caught her shoulders and pushed her at arm's length, surprising himself as well as her.

"What do you think you're doing?" he demanded breathlessly.

She looked back at him in all apparent innocence. Her cheeks were flushed, her eyes bright. "I thought we were proving your theory that you don't have to be emotionally involved to enjoy a kiss."

That hadn't been emotion, he told himself. The racing blood and lack of breath had been simply lust. True, that didn't usually happen during a simple kiss, but then, as he'd reminded himself earlier, he had very little experience of virgins. Her innocence probably did provide an added stimulus that had taken him by surprise.

His world righted itself. He was able to ask her, his control in place again, "And *did* you?"

She looked into his eyes. Deeply. He knew what she was looking for and did his best to hide it.

Then, his control rocking a little, he realized that that meant he *had* felt something if he had to hide it. He dropped his hands from her and rested them on his hips. Breaking the contact *had* to help.

She sighed, and he thought he saw a trace of defeat in the gesture. But her gaze lingered on him as though she didn't entirely believe his pose.

"I can't answer that," she said finally. "I seem to have compromised the test."

"How so?"

Her gaze changed from skepticism to self-effacing candor. "I was more emotionally involved than I expected to be. Maybe we can try it again another time. I'm sure you'll become so disagreeable to me before this tour is over that I'll be able to stay within the parameters of the test. Good night, Gib."

Kathy turned toward her room and saw her mother standing in the suite's open doorway, a bright plaid scarf draped over the shoulder of a dark blue dress. Her mouth was open.

Kathy went into her room without saying a word.

She didn't know how long her mother had been standing there, but past experience had taught her that her mother never missed anything. She was bound to have seen it all—Kathy's wholehearted involvement in a kiss shared with the man who was supposed to be her protection on a tour that was devoted to promoting her book and on the advantages of virginity!

She locked her door and paced around the king-size bed with its opulent red-and-gold-paisley bedspread. It was just a kiss. No reason to be concerned. It was just the first time a kiss had that much impact on her senses, on her emotions.

She wrapped her arms around herself, remembering Gib's arms wrapped around her. It was curious, she thought, that he represented everything she opposed and still his embrace had felt like a haven.

She hadn't thought that could happen. She'd embarked on the kiss-test simply to prove to him that he'd find no enjoyment in it with her if she wasn't emotionally involved.

Instead, she'd become involved—with the man who shouldn't have appealed to her at all.

She felt the whole foundation of her philosophy on sexual relationships wobble. Mostly because she'd realized how small a step it would have taken from her involvement in that kiss to a passionate entanglement much more difficult to walk away from.

"YOU LOOK a little shaken, Gilbert." Patsy sat on one of the stools at the breakfast bar and watched him pour coffee into a cup. He struggled to operate calmly, as though nothing unusual had happened.

He held up the pot. "I just need a cup of coffee. Want to join me?"

She gave him the same skeptical look Kathy had given him just a moment ago. "No, thank you. I had one glass of Vouvray and I'm quite clearheaded. Can you make the same claim?"

He smiled at her and replaced the pot on the warmer. "Always."

He carried his cup to the sofa, and she followed him.

"You know," she said, sitting in the chair opposite him, "when your aunts took me through their rose garden that afternoon, when you were introduced to Kathy and me, I told them that I liked the idea of a bodyguard and that I liked you. But I expressed a little concern that a handsome young man along on this trip might be more of a threat to Kathy's stand than a benefit." She crossed her legs and tugged the scarf off her shoulder. "They told me I had nothing to fear, that you don't believe in love and have no use for virgins because for you, sex is simply recreation."

He took a sip of coffee. Everything she said was true, he just never realized before how useless it made him sound.

"That's right," he said.

Her expression changed suddenly from amiable matron to protective mother. "I feel obliged to warn you that if you intend to use my daughter as recreation, I'll cut your heart out with a pineapple corer."

He put his cup down and raised an eyebrow. "Now, there's a picture. I promise you, those are not my intentions, but if they were, you don't give

Kathy enough credit. She's already told me she can't be shaken from what she believes."

"And she believes that," Patsy said, meticulously folding the colorful scarf. Then she looked at him over it. "Because she's never been in love. She's a woman, not a child, and in every other way she's the smartest woman I know. But she's never loved a man, and she doesn't know how vulnerable that can make you. I want this tour to be her chance for recognition and financial security. Don't you dare ruin it for her by making a liar out of her."

He tried to remember why he'd rejected Browning's offer of employment. And why he'd let his aunts talk him into this particular duty.

"You misjudge me, Patsy," he said simply.

Kathy's bedroom door burst open, and she came as far as the sofa to stand halfway between it and the chair. She frowned impatiently at Patsy.

"If I hear this kind of discussion between the two of you one more time," she threatened, "I'll ship both of you back to Boston and continue on my own! You think because I've never been to bed with a man that I have to be protected like some pubescent little teen or I'll swoon all over the first man who appeals to me and bed him for the experience? Thanks a lot, Mom." She glowered from Patsy to Gib, then focused on her mother again. "I instigated that kiss because I was trying to make a point. Instead, I learned a little something from it. But, Good Lord, I'm twenty-six. I have a brain. I can feel something without letting it control what I do about it."

Her temper apparently spent, she folded her arms, glowered again, then stalked into the little kitchen and poured herself a cup of coffee.

Patsy caught Gib's eye. He noticed that hers were twinkling.

"I'm afraid we can't apologize, darling," she said, raising her voice to be heard in the kitchen. "It's my job by nature to look out for you, and Gib's been hired to do the same thing. You can't escape."

Kathy returned to the spot of her last oratory and replied, her voice a little quieter, "Then don't assume I'm a witless imbecile. I can understand *him* making that mistake." She glanced at *him* with toxic disapproval. "But I don't understand it from you."

She marched off to her room.

Patsy got wearily to her feet. "I guess she told us," she said.

Gib stood and offered her a helping hand. "You, particularly."

"I noticed. But I advise you not to rub it in."

"Of course not."

She met his gaze, and this time they shared a kind of comraderie. Both were committed to the protection of a woman bent on evading them.

Patsy patted the hand with which he'd helped her up. "Good night, Gib."

She disappeared into her room, and Gib sank back onto the sofa with a groan. Two days down out of twenty-eight. He wasn't going to make it. Alligator wrestling would be easier than this.

"IT HAS PROPELLERS!" Kathy stared in shock at the commuter plane scheduled to fly them to New York. All the other passengers had boarded, and Patsy was now chatting amiably with the copilot, who was helping her up the small flight of stairs.

Gib stopped at the bottom of the stairway when

he realized that was genuine distress on Kathy's face. She looked delicious in a camel-colored slacks suit, a green blouse visible at the neck.

He went back to her, not entirely sure what the problem was. "Yes. Propellers. They make the plane go and keep it up."

She still stared at them. He saw her swallow. "I thought everybody used jets." She looked down at him, fear now clearly visible in her eyes. "I mean, you hear about executive jets, don't you? Those are small—"

"Propellers are generally more efficient on a smaller plane landing on a smaller runway."

"But this is Logan Airport. And we're going to La Guardia! Neither one's a small airport."

"This plane probably goes to other smaller airports all over New England."

"Oh." She looked at the propellers again, then back at him, fear replaced by a sense of humor. "Of course. I'm sure raising two fans in the air and expecting it to support many tons of steel is a very sound principle."

He put an arm around her shoulders and urged her toward the stairs. "I'm not a physicist, but the principle has worked for a long time."

She stopped on the second stair, her sense of humor slipping. "Except for those times when it hasn't."

"That happens to jets, too," he pointed out gently. "And everything else that moves."

She walked up the stairs and found their seats. They were side by side, and Patsy sat behind them beside a young man in a three-piece suit already hard at work on a laptop. She looked at them mournfully over the backs of their seats, clearly unhappy that she'd be getting no conversation from her companion.

"You take the window seat," Kathy said when Gib tried to urge her toward it. "I'd rather sit on the aisle."

"You've never flown before?" he asked.

"Twice," she replied as she sat down and buckled her seat belt. "Once to L.A. with a college roommate and once to Miami with friends. But both times were on a jet. It's not going to take us forever to get there, is it?"

He sat and buckled his own belt. "Forty minutes. It'll be over before you know it. Want to hold my hand?" He held it toward her, palm upward.

She studied it, then him with a wry expression. "You're a bodyguard. I don't think the job requires that you protect me from my own fears."

"I'm not making the offer as your bodyguard." He heard the words come out of his mouth and wondered what had prompted him to say *that.*

She was looking at him with that interest that always snared his awareness and stole his breath. After a lifetime of parents and multiple stepparents who'd hardly noticed him, and women who treated him with the same casualness with which he treated them, finding that he had the ability to fascinate someone was completely unsettling.

"Who are you making the offer for?" she asked, then considered what she'd said and corrected herself. "As?"

"A friend," he said. The look in her eyes softened, and he added theatrically, so that she didn't take him too seriously, "Just another traveler on the tour of life."

Instead of taking his hand, she tucked her arm in his and held on—for every one of the forty minutes.

At the terminal he collected their bags and found the limo Cordelia had hired to drive them to their appointments over the next three days. The driver, a large African-American man with a brilliant smile, introduced himself as Clarence. He wore the gray livery of the company he represented.

He drove them to their Manhattan hotel, signaled a bellman to help with their luggage and wanted to know what time he was to return. "I understand Miss McQuade has a press conference, but my schedule doesn't tell me where."

"It's here at the hotel," Gib replied. "But we'll be going out to dinner about seven."

"Very good. I'll be here."

In the suite, a plush, cheerful set of rooms decorated in yellow and gray, Kathy sat on a wicker sofa in the living room and kicked off her shoes as she consulted her schedule.

"What happens at a press conference, anyway?" she asked Gib. "I mean, I know generally what goes on, but who's there, and do I speak, or do I just answer questions?"

"Someone from the publicity firm Cordelia hired will stop by an hour before the conference and give you a little coaching." Gib checked out the usual small kitchen and found a drawer filled with packets of ground coffee. There was even a bottle of Irish cream in the small refrigerator. "You can make a statement if you want to, or you can just let the press ask you questions. All the local radio, television and print media will be here, possibly some national news people and wire services.''

She nodded. Apparently she'd gotten over serious stage fright after the TV appearance in Boston. Or maybe surviving the flight on a plane with propellers gave her new courage. Whatever the reason, she headed off for her bedroom, humming a tune.

Bindle Communications sent a small, slender brunette in a navy blue suit and small gold hoops at her ears.

''Andrea Asante,'' she said confidently, offering Gib her hand as he opened the door for her.

''Gib London.'' He shook her hand, then gestured her toward the wicker sofa and chairs. ''Kathy will be right out.''

''London?'' She placed a folder on the glass coffee table on a wicker stand and sat on the sofa. ''You represent the publisher?''

''Yes.''

She didn't seem to like that. ''You and—'' she consulted something in her folder ''—Kathy McQuade are traveling together?''

''Yes.'' He couldn't see what she was getting at until she hit him over the head with it.

''But she's claiming to be a virgin. How is it going to look as she travels from city to city with a hunk in tow?''

''Miss Asante—'' Before Gib could reply, Kathy came out of her room, dressed for her press conference in a green dress with a high collar. It clung to breast and hip in a way that was both flattering and seductive. His heart stalled.

Andrea stood, and Kathy reached across the table to shake her hand. ''I'm Kathy McQuade. I claim to be a virgin because I am, and I'm certain Gib London has never been towed by any woman.'' She cast him a rueful glance. She was clearly in top form this afternoon. She took a chair opposite Andrea and folded her hands in her lap. ''My mother's with us. She's in the shower right now, playing with the built-in soap and shampoo dispensers. Gib said you'd have some advice for me?''

Gib went to make a pot of coffee, silently enjoying the way Kathy took control of the preparation session from the woman who was supposed to be an expert at it.

Andrea coached her on how to turn tricky questions around, how to choose her words carefully to put the best spin on an answer bound to be unpopular, how to maintain the best possible appearance in the face of rudeness or ridicule. ''The press isn't known for its courtesy,'' she said, wiggling a pen between her first two fingers, ''and, let's face it, your opinions are bound to generate a little hostility.''

Gib leaned against the counter with his third cup of coffee and watched Kathy lean back in her chair. ''Hostility?'' she asked, clearly surprised.

''Women have worked hard to get where they are,'' Andrea answered, tucking things tidily into her folder, apparently feeling some of that hostility herself. ''And your ideas are pushing them back into the fifties again.''

''By suggesting that they take control of their lives?''

''By suggesting that they can only assume control of their lives when someone else has control of their bodies.''

Kathy had apparently been listening when Andrea

told her how to maintain her dignity in the face of direct opposition. She pointed out calmly, "When a woman says no to sex that she doesn't feel is safe or timely or comfortable for her for whatever reason, she *has* control over her body."

Andrea looked directly at her. "No. She has control when she can do whatever the hell she wants whenever she wants without having to answer to a parent or a church or some moral majority that thinks it has the right to decide what she should or shouldn't do."

Kathy recrossed her legs as though the action helped her rethink her approach. "Did you get where you are professionally without putting disciplines in place in your life?"

"We're talking about a personal life," Andrea responded.

"Yes, we are. And that's infinitely more important than work and therefore needs more care, more attention, more *thought* before you make decisions that will affect all the rest of it."

Andrea smiled scornfully and shook her head. "Our lives are restricted everywhere we turn by laws of one kind or another. All we have left are each other's arms. Can't we at least have that?"

"Romantically put," Kathy replied, her voice still calm but just a shade higher, tighter. "And that would make sense if it didn't have the potential to make you sick, make you pregnant or kill you."

Andrea stood, looping her purse over her shoulder and tucking her folder under her arm. "Good luck at the conference," she said politely, if a little stiffly. "I'll be distributing your press kit, then I'll be in the back row if there's anything you need."

Kathy walked her to the door and out of Gib's line of vision. "Thank you," he heard Kathy say with the same rigid courtesy. "I appreciate your help. And your honesty."

"Well. You're living in a dreamworld, girl."

"I thought life and love were all about dreams," Kathy said.

Gib heard a chuckle that was almost affectionate. "You are hopeless. And tell London to keep his distance, or everyone will get the wrong idea."

The door closed.

Kathy walked into the kitchen, poured a cup of coffee and took a long sip. Then she winced. "What's in this?"

"It's a French roast," he answered. "Too strong?"

"Possibly. I can feel my hair standing up." But she took another sip.

He laughed lightly. "Andrea's probably responsible for that. You okay?"

She looked surprised by the question. "Of course I am. You don't think I've never met opposition before? I'm traveling around with you, remember?"

"But I've been trying to keep my opinions to myself."

"And I appreciate that." She took another deep swig, then put her cup down on the counter with a little bang. "So, here I go to face the press, with my bodyguard and my publicity director set squarely against me. This should be an interesting afternoon."

She smiled dryly and turned toward her bedroom. "I'd at least better make sure my breath is minty fresh."

GIB STAYED in the background, knowing Andrea's suggestion was a sensible one, sitting at the opposite end of the back row Andrea occupied. Patsy sat beside him.

Kathy glowed, even across the distance of the hotel meeting room. The hotel's conference director told him he'd originally set a smaller room for the meeting, but as the press began to arrive he'd had to open the sliding doors into the adjoining room.

Gib guessed that sixty or more separate press entities were represented along with their respective sound and camera crews. Questions were shouted, strobes flashed, playful taunts were thrown at Kathy, but she met everything with a smile and an answer that at first had caused buzzes of conversation, light laughter, but eventually respectful silence.

He would wager that few of the men and women there agreed with her, but a half hour into the conference, their questions became more serious and intelligent than playful.

"I'd appreciate it," she told them finally, after an hour and a half of questions, "if you would make it clear in your reports that I don't fault any adult who makes other choices for whatever reason. I just think it's important that young women know that it's okay to be celibate. And more mature women, too. They have the right to think about themselves before they think about the needs of a potential partner. We've come to believe there's something wrong with a man or woman who isn't eager to take advantage of our more liberal attitudes, that it makes us somehow less generous. I don't think that's true. Sex isn't the only way to communicate, to offer love and friendship, but it's the one that has the most potential to affect your future."

There was a last-minute question, a few more photos, then the group began to disperse.

"That went well," Patsy said with a sigh of relief. "I know she's a big girl, but I'm always so afraid she's going to get ripped apart."

Gib was gaining new respect for Kathy, even if he did consider her point of view naive. "She holds her own very well. And she has a confident presence. That sets an impression before she even opens her mouth."

AS PEOPLE and equipment streamed toward the exit, Kathy picked up her purse and noticed Andrea across the room in smiling conversation with a man in jeans and a leather jacket. He'd identified himself during the conference as a reporter from the *Village View*. Then she saw the man's arm go around Andrea. She leaned into him and they shared a kiss that suggested there was a lot more between them than professional acquaintance. Kathy realized what had brought on Andrea's defensive attitude toward Kathy's book in spite of all assurances that she held a live-and-let-live policy.

The reporter said something that brought disappointment to Andrea's face and what seemed to be a plea of some sort. She wrapped her arms around his neck and looking into his eyes, spoke earnestly.

He responded with the same earnestness, shaking his head and shrugging, as though expressing helplessness. Then he withdrew her arms from around his neck, kissed each of her hands, then walked away.

Andrea watched him go, her shoulders sagging. She finally turned back to the table on which she'd set out Kathy's publicity folders and pulled a cardboard file box out from under it. She began to pack up the leftover materials.

"The professional communicator," Gib observed, coming up beside Kathy, "seems to be having trouble communicating."

"Before the conference started," Kathy said, frowning in Andrea's direction, "she told me she had a hot date tonight. I wonder if it was with him? And I wonder if it's been canceled?"

Gib nodded speculatively. "She looks upset about something. Clarence is waiting." He pointed toward the doors where Clarence was laughing with her mother. "Ready to go to dinner?"

Kathy watched Andrea work, everything about her from her chic suit to her short but stylish hairstyle reflecting the image of the professional woman climbing the ladder of success.

But it was the other part of her Kathy related to. The shoulders of the chic suit had a decidedly dispirited air, and Andrea kept tucking the right side of her hair behind her ear though it remained perfectly in place. Kathy guessed it was an attempt to appear casual and unaffected by something that had definitely affected her.

Kathy glanced up at Gib. "Do you have any objections to my inviting Andrea to join us?"

He smiled, looking confused. "No, I don't. But do you want discord at the dinner table when you've just spent almost two hours with the press?"

"The conference is over," Kathy replied. "We'll talk about something else."

"Go ahead. I'll wait for you by the door."

Andrea blinked at Kathy as she put the last folder in the box. "Pardon me?"

"I wondered if we could take you to dinner with us," Kathy asked. "You must have put in a long day, too. And we won't talk about sex, premarital or otherwise."

"Um..." Andrea blinked again, looked around herself as though suddenly unfamiliar with her surroundings, then indicated the box of materials. "I have this stuff..."

"Do you have a car?"

"No, I came from the office in a cab."

"Well, we'll just put it in the limo, then drop you off at home afterward."

Andrea nodded. "Okay," she said with an uncertainty that rang through despite her nod.

Chapter Five

Clarence drove his party to Le Rivage on Andrea's suggestion. "Jay and I love the bistro fare there," she said. "It's the best French buy in the Theater District."

"Is Jay the reporter who looks at you as though you're his personal angel?" Patsy asked. She and Andrea sat side by side in the seat facing Kathy and Gib. When Andrea appeared surprised by the question, Patsy added with a smile, "I saw the two of you after the conference. I thought you'd be leaving together."

Andrea nodded. "We've been together a couple of months. But our schedules have been so busy this week that we've hardly seen each other. We'd planned to have dinner tonight, but he has to file his story."

"Merging two careers is one of the most serious threats to romance, according to all the talk shows."

"Oh, I don't think so." Andrea fussed with the right side of her hair. "It's a challenge, of course, but we're committed to each other." She gave Kathy a look that was half apologetic, half aggressive.

"Even without formal vows exchanged. Love keeps us together, not a marriage license."

"You're lucky to have such a relationship," Kathy said, "However it works."

Over dinner Kathy discovered that Andrea had spent a year at Boston College, and that they had some friends in common. The atmosphere warmed between as they talked nonstop, comparing notes and catching up on who was working where, who'd gotten married, who had children.

"Paula Sullivan had triplets!" Andrea announced with a squeal that would have been completely out of character for the woman who'd arrived at the hotel suite that afternoon. "She was working on her Ph.D. in English literature at Cornell and met this man who does these fitness seminars. He was a gold medalist in the high jump in Barcelona in '92. Anyway. Three boys!"

"No!"

"Yes. Can you imagine fitting three babies around your dissertation? Not me. And Jay's in complete agreement. Later. Much later."

"Well, not *too* much later," Patsy put in.

"I'd like to have a vice presidency first," Andrea said seriously, "and Jay wants a column. Of course, by then we'll have a house in Connecticut, a—" She stopped abruptly, her face going white, her eyes widening at something above Patsy's head.

"What?" Patsy asked Gib anxiously. "I've sprouted horns after all, haven't I?"

Gib turned to look over his shoulder just as Kathy spotted the man coming out of the lounge and heading for the door, a small, clingy blonde on his arm behaving as though she was quite accustomed to being there—and not in a platonic way.

He was the man Kathy had seen Andrea with after the press conference. The one to whom Andrea claimed to be committed without need of a marriage license, and who'd canceled their plans for dinner because he'd had to file his story.

Jay, his eyes on the blonde as they walked slowly toward the door, literally hanging on each other, didn't notice Andrea staring at him from several tables away.

Andrea put a hand to her heart and drew a breath that sounded strangled.

"Ladies' room?" Kathy asked quickly, pushing back her chair.

Andrea's answer was another strangled breath.

Kathy and Patsy took matters into their own hands and led her between them to the rest room as Gib went to take care of the check and find Clarence.

Kathy sat Andrea on a stool turned away from the wall of makeup mirrors and dabbed water on her face with a paper towel while Patsy massaged Andrea's shoulders.

Andrea stared into space, her eyes miserable and spilling tears. Kathy and Patsy continued their ministrations for ten minutes until Andrea stopped sobbing.

Then they found a corridor off the rest rooms that led to the rear entrance where Gib waited.

"How did you know we'd come out this way?" Kathy asked.

"I didn't," he replied with a candid smile. "I've got Clarence waiting in the front. Come on. Limo's right here. I'll get Clarence."

They were on their way through the neon-lit night in a matter of minutes. Kathy sat beside Andrea, an arm around her shoulders.

"Well, I look silly, don't I," Andrea said, pressing a soggy tissue to her nose. "After all that talk about Jay being committed to me without benefit of marriage."

"That doesn't have anything to do with it," Kathy said, handing her a fresh tissue from the pocket pack in her purse. "The marriage license certainly doesn't guarantee fidelity. If a man isn't inclined to be faithful to the woman he claims to love, a wedding won't make any difference."

"I don't understand him," Andrea said, her face crumpling anew. She sobbed for a few moments, then drew a breath and demanded tearfully, "Wouldn't it be easier to just tell me he doesn't love me anymore? I mean, didn't it occur to him that I might see them, or someone we both know might see them? What's the point of pretending to me?"

"Because there's something about you he admires," Gib said quietly, "that he doesn't get from her."

The three women turned to him in indignation.

He raised both hands in a gesture of peace. "I don't approve. I'm just offering a possible explanation. My father had quite an entanglement going, while he was married to his third wife, that involved his secretary and a cookbook author."

The women's expressions transformed with interest. Even Clarence adjusted the rearview mirror.

"My stepmother was a beautiful woman and looked wonderful on his arm at parties," he explained. "Dad's secretary kept his life organized, and he really needed that. The cookbook author made wonderful manicotti, a favorite of his, and lent a sort of coziness to a couple of evenings a week that he didn't get from his secretary or his wife."

"That's barbaric!" Kathy declared.

"How long did it last?" Patsy wanted to know.

"Not long," Gib replied. "I happened to be home for spring break because my mother was honeymooning with husband number two in Barbados. It all fell apart one sunny afternoon when the cookbook author somehow misunderstood the gossip columns and thought my *stepmother* was in Barbados when she was really upstairs, sorting through her wardrobe to donate some things to charity and discovered an unfamiliar scent on one of her dressing gowns—Dad's secretary's scent."

Patsy winced. "Did your father survive?"

Gib nodded. "But then he walked with a limp."

"And your point is," Kathy asked defensively, "that we're not intended to be monogamous?"

"No, that's not what I mean. Although, every experience in the lives of my parents would validate that. I'm just suggesting that Jay's motivation for fooling around on Andrea might be the same as Dad's. Andrea's steady and solid and working with him toward his goals, while the blonde looked like the type who demands nothing from him except that he be a guy."

Kathy looked at her mother, then at Andrea. "How are we expected to conduct relationships with a species that thinks that way?"

"Maybe we're not," Andrea said mournfully, drying her eyes. "Maybe Gib's father has the right idea."

"My husband and I had a wonderful marriage." Patsy leaned into her corner thoughtfully. "The only thing wrong with it was that it lasted only ten years."

"He...died?" Andrea asked.

"Sudden heart attack. But he was loving and faithful and everything I could ever hope to find in a lifelong companion. So, it can work. You just have to find a man who'll stay."

"That's a tall order apparently," Andrea observed with a sniff.

"That's what makes love so special." Patsy winked at Andrea. "And when you find it, you usually know it, and you treat it that way."

"Here we are, Miss Asante." Clarence pulled up in front of an apartment building on a quiet street lined with small trees.

"I'll walk you in." Gib stepped out as Clarence came around to open the door, ignoring Andrea's protests.

Kathy and Patsy waited silently as Gib walked Andrea up to her apartment.

Clarence, still positioned at the limo's back door, pulled it open when Gib returned five minutes later. Then they were on their way again to the hotel, a solemn trio in the back of the plush limousine.

In the suite, Patsy said good-night and went to her room while Gib made another pot of coffee.

"Could you use something other than the French roast?" Kathy asked, studying the drawer filled with packets of coffee. She looked at him hopefully. "I don't suppose I could interest you in hazelnut cream?"

He rolled his eyes but took the packet from her

and ripped it open. "That's a little pantywaist for me, but okay."

Kathy kicked off her shoes and hiked up onto the small square of counter across from him and watched him work. "Your childhood must have been pretty difficult," she said.

He waited until he'd filled the carafe with water, then poured it into the coffeemaker's reservoir before answering her.

"In some ways," he replied, trying to remember exactly what he'd felt then. He was a little foggy on some of the details. As a teenager he'd made a few imaginary adjustments on what he remembered, and sometimes now it was hard to separate fact from his personal fiction. "I had far fewer restrictions on me than other children because my parents were so involved in their either hot-and-new, or old-and-decaying relationships that they tended to forget I was around."

"That's terrible," she sympathized.

He pushed the coffee basket into place and turned on the coffeemaker. "It was sometimes. It was hard to get serious advice on anything, because no one knew me well enough to give it. And it was hard to get comfort for the same reason." He turned to find her light blue eyes filled with sympathy for him. That both annoyed and touched him. He leaned against the counter behind him and folded his arms. "On the other hand, I got everything I ever asked for because it kept me out of the way. I got to go to great places, to overnights with friends, on vacations with the families of roommates at school, to friends' homes for holidays when I was in college. And my mother had a preference for tropical locations when she was getting married, or getting divorced, or recovering from either one, so visiting her usually meant swimming, surfing, scuba diving..." He grinned. "Meeting women in bikinis."

Kathy studied him closely, as though trying to see beyond his clever answers and into his heart.

But he permitted no one to look there.

"It did hurt once," he admitted candidly, hoping that would be enough to satisfy her. Actually, it was a colossal understatement. "But your life is your life and you learn to accept it, even when you're just a little kid. And some pretty wonderful people came through my life, a cook-housekeeper, a couple of teachers who were very special, a sergeant in boot camp, my aunts. All in all, I know I've been very lucky."

"Are your parents still alive?"

A moment's careful control and he could answer that. "No. My mother and husband number three died in a traffic accident on a mountain road in Monaco a number of years ago. My father died of cancer two years ago."

"I'm sorry," Kathy said softly.

"It's over." Satisfied that he'd wrapped up his past in a very sane package, he smiled at her, certain she'd accept it as such. It was more than he'd ever told anyone.

But she rested her elbows on her stockinged knees, her dress drawn up to mid-thigh by her position on the counter, and leaned toward him across the narrow kitchen. "I admire the way you don't fault anyone," she said, a little frown between her eyebrows, "but do you think you'll ever be able to love anyone?"

What *was* it with her? She didn't need anyone to guard her body. If it was as hard as her head, she'd be impervious to injury.

But he'd held her only yesterday. He knew her body wasn't hard at all. It was soft and small and fragrant. And that knowledge left him at a vulnerable disadvantage and inclined to spill his guts. But he swallowed instead and drew a breath.

"Not the way you envision love," he replied honestly. "Because I don't believe it exists that way."

"But the world is filled with other examples besides your parents. I mean, even if you believe the current statistics about fifty percent of marriages ending in divorce, that's still half that succeed. That's millions of people who manage to stay together and keep loving each other."

"Maybe. But they're probably a lot different from me."

Her eyes still held his with her complete attention. He was beginning to find it a little unnerving.

"Are you afraid," she asked gently, "that there's no love in your heart? Is that why you never try to give it?"

That was it. His customary cool abandoned him completely. He straightened away from the counter and reached above her to open a cupboard, putting a hand to the top of her head to protect it.

"You know," he said a little hotly, "I'm not some lab experiment you can dissect and analyze then calmly create theories about. I've told you all I want you to know." He banged both cups on the counter and checked the pot. It was still dripping the sweet-smelling, pantywaist coffee. "You like to keep your body to yourself—" he pointed a finger at her, then one at his own chest "—I like to keep my feelings to myself. How would *you* like it if I was continually trying to get you into bed?"

Kathy lowered her eyes so they wouldn't betray her. She'd never known anyone before who made the idea of joining him in bed so appealing. So this was what the temptation felt like. It wasn't a mighty passion, or a desperate yearning, but just a very enticing possibility—one of those forks in life's road that gave you the feeling you'd always regret it if you went the other way.

But the whole point of her book, of her philosophy, was that satisfying curiosity wasn't what life was intended to be about. At least, not exclusively.

And she'd learned something here. She'd been right about him. He *was* afraid he didn't have love in him.

"You know what I'm going to do?" he asked. He'd moved to stand in front of her, one hand on the counter on either side of her. His hazel eyes were turbulent with an emotion that looked like anger but seemed to be more complex.

She guessed that it meant he didn't have control of the moment, and he didn't like that.

He wasn't touching her, but he was close enough that she could feel the heat from his body, smell his cologne and the laundry-soap freshness of his dress shirt.

Air tried to evacuate her lungs but seemed to entangle itself; she felt as though a large knot was stuck in her chest.

"What?" she asked, her voice thin as it slid past the knot.

"Every time you invade my space," he threatened, "I'll invade yours. You get personal with me, and I'll kiss you."

Horrors, she thought dryly, dropping her lashes so that he wouldn't see her looking hopeful. "And that's to prove what?" she asked calmly. "That you have no love in you? Or that you have no use for virgins? If you ask me, it contradicts both."

He put a hand to the back of her head and carried out his threat. Punitively at first—and for about five seconds—and then with a delicious tenderness that served to destroy whatever negative impression he'd intended to create with it and instead left her limp and wanting more.

He took a fistful of her hair and drew her away far enough so he could look into her eyes. "I *didn't* ask you," he said, then freed her, poured his coffee and walked off to his room.

Kathy sat there, everything inside her quaking at the realization that on this tour to promote her book on virginity she was faced with the first real threat to it she'd ever experienced.

IN ORLANDO, FLORIDA, Kathy was invited to speak to several private high schools and church youth groups, besides keeping her appointments with radio and television stations and meeting with newspaper reporters.

"But it's so *difficult,*" one nice-looking young man in the assembly of young people in a Catholic high school auditorium said from the middle of the crowd.

Kathy guessed from the way the other teenagers reacted to him that he was popular and admired.

"I mean, you know, we have feelings. We're not

little kids who don't think about the future. We do. But anything could get us tomorrow—cancer, the bomb, El Nino.'' The other young people were respectfully silent through his first two examples, then dissolved into laughter at the third. ''So, if we have protection, why can't we enjoy today?''

The kids chanted his name. ''Tra-vis! Tra-vis!''

''Because the only foolproof protection is abstinence,'' she replied confidently, knowing she had to appear confident or lose this group entirely, ''and a smart man like you shouldn't trust his future to chance. And while it's true that no one can guarantee you a future, if you do get to have one, do you want it compromised by a child you're not ready for or a disease that can't be cured?''

''But what if you *don't* have a future?'' someone shouted out. ''You've wasted today.''

''No, you haven't!'' she shouted back. ''If you abstain from sex until you're ready, you've offered your friendship, your concern, your sense of responsibility to someone you care about, and you've made a hero of yourself.''

There was laughter at the word *hero,* a little murmur of scorn at the suggestion that lack of sexual activity did not mean loss.

''Okay, look,'' she said, walking down the stage steps and to the top of the middle aisle. She saw kids leaning around one another to keep sight of her. ''Travis says you're not children, and I can see that, because you're listening. Well, think about this. Using your brains and keeping your futures safe from some of the things that can destroy it, is adult decision making, big-time. The choices don't come any tougher than that.'' She raised her left hand. ''An hour's pleasure..." The boys were mumbling and laughing and shoving at Travis's shoulder.

Kathy laughed. "Okay. For some of you, maybe two hours." Then she raised her right hand. "Against your entire lifetime lived the way you see it right now. What are your dreams? CEO of a major corporation? Rock star? Trucker? Surgeon? Clothes designer? It'll be a lot harder to get there as a single parent with a baby and bills to pay. And you won't live to get there if you catch something fatal."

The entire room was now silent.

Kathy looked out on the crowd of attentive faces and realized in surprise that her exchange with these kids had ceased to be about her book and was now about their lives.

She saw the wit and intelligence in their faces, the dreams in their eyes, the character and the promise. She felt an urgent need to shadow every single one of them into his or her twenties and see that they got where they wanted to go.

"All I ask is that you think first," she pleaded with them. "Make that your motto. The next time you're tempted to have sex, think first, 'This moment or the rest of my life?'"

Gib stood in the wings, and Kathy walked toward him, completely drained of energy and endurance. She'd had two television appearances yesterday, a radio interview this morning, and she'd spoken to another group of young people before this one.

The school's principal, an older nun in a simple blue skirt and white blouse, came to shake Kathy's hand. She was beaming. "Thank you!" she said effusively. "I've said that over and over, though never quite as eloquently or convincingly. And of course—'' the nun grinned ''—young people think nuns are born in a veil and completely without sexuality, so it's no big deal for us to be celibate. But to hear it from someone young and beautiful, hopefully it'll take root. Bless you.''

Kathy hugged her. ''Thank you, Mother Anne. I got rather involved there. I feel as though I have to follow them personally and keep them from harm.''

The nun hugged her in return. ''I know. That's the curse of working with young people. You know how to protect little children, but once they're free to strike out on their own, you can only hope you've prepared them.'' She held Kathy at arm's length. ''Your mother tells me you've always been very special.''

Kathy waved that thought away. ''She's the type who bored friends with pictures of me all the time I was growing up. Now that I'm getting a little publicity, she's out of control.''

The nun met her eyes. ''She says your intention was to use the money from this book to clear away her debt. You're a very generous young woman.''

''She's a very special mother. Where is she, anyway?''

''She's visiting with the sisters in the cafeteria. She said she'd meet you at the limousine.'' Mother Anne hugged Kathy again, then shook Gib's hand. ''We'll pray for your safety on the rest of your tour, and for your happiness.''

''Thank you, Mother.''

Gib and Kathy walked side by side to the limousine where Patsy sat in the front, chatting with the driver.

They returned to a bungalow set back in a garden

on the grounds of a hotel and convention center complex.

"Let's go to Disney World!" Patsy proposed, her eyes bright with anticipation. "The hotel's sending a shuttle tonight. We could have dinner there and try the rides."

It was the last thing Kathy felt like doing at the moment, but possibly after a nap…

"If I can have an hour in the sun on a chaise longue," Kathy bargained, "I think I could muster the energy."

"I could go myself." Patsy pinched her cheek. "But you've been working so hard. You need some fun." She shooed her toward her room. "Okay. Change into something for sunbathing, and I'll answer the phone and keep everyone else at bay."

When Kathy walked out of her bedroom in shorts and a tank top she'd packed especially for the few days in Florida, Gib was on the flagstone patio in nothing but white tennis shorts, setting up two chairs.

"What are you doing?" she asked a little testily. She didn't want to argue about anything for an hour.

He seemed surprised by the question. "I can't guard you from inside."

"I don't want to fight about anything," she warned him.

"Then don't start anything. I won't say a word."

"All right."

"All right."

They lay side by side in the sun for half an hour. Gib had placed the chairs close enough that if she reached out a hand she'd be able to touch his. She was surprised by how tempting that notion was.

"I can't believe we're into the second week of the tour already," she said, deciding that reaching out with the sound of her voice was safer.

"Time flies when you're having fun," he replied, eyes closed, voice lazy.

"How can you guard me with your eyes closed?" she asked, propping up on an elbow.

"If you scream," he replied, "I'll know you're in trouble."

"I could be gone by the time you open your eyes, kidnapped by some white slaver intent on selling me to some Arab prince."

He smiled without opening his eyes. "Your next book should be fiction. Actually, I have very good ears. I can hear an iguana under your chair right now."

With a disbelieving huff, Kathy turned to look under her chair, discovered there was indeed a lizard under it, screamed, kicked both legs in the air in a vain attempt to get out of the chair and managed only to tilt it toward Gib as she shifted her weight.

He leaned toward her as she fell, trying to catch her, but succeeding only in collapsing his own chair.

She lay under him a moment later on the warm flagstone, her eyes shut tightly.

"Tell me," she pleaded, "that there's not a mushed iguana under me."

Gib laughed lightly. "He darted off at the first sign of trouble."

Kathy opened her eyes and looked into his. They were lazy and laughing.

"Don't like lizards?" he asked.

"No," she replied, aware suddenly that she could feel his warm skin against hers in a dozen places along her body. She tried to think of other things. "I thought iguanas lived in Mexico."

"I suppose they're happy wherever it's tropical. They live in Cuba, too. Maybe this guy was imported."

"You didn't really *hear* the lizard, did you?"

"No. I'd glanced at you a minute before you opened your eyes and saw him lying there in your shade. He wasn't hurting anything, so I didn't tell you."

"That was a dirty trick."

"I've got a million of them."

"Oh, you do not. You put on this tough-guy, can't-reach-me-with-a-yardstick performance, and you're really just an old softie."

Except that he wasn't—at least not everywhere.

The lazy expression in his eyes changed subtly. "You've wandered into my space again."

She pretended dismay. "Good heavens. You must be broadening your borders."

But he wouldn't be distracted. He kissed her gently, sweetly, and she suspected her remark hadn't really annoyed him at all.

She kissed him back to show him that he shouldn't toy with her that way if he knew what was good for him, but apparently he didn't. The kiss went on and on, until he finally groaned, pushed himself to his feet and offered her both his hands to pull her to hers.

"What's this about your mother's debts?" he asked, righting her chair and then his own.

She ignored the chair and went to study a small palm tree that leaned gracefully out of its pot as though trying to see over the stone wall that surrounded the patio. She told him about Jack Trent and her suspicions about what he'd stolen, and her mother's unwillingness to file charges against him. She went back to her chair with an angry frown. "She's convinced he's coming back, but even if he did, I don't see what good that'll do her."

Gib lay back in his chair. "Was she in love with him?"

"I think so. She never said she was, but why else would she refuse to blame him? She's acting like a lovesick victim."

"If she loves him—"

"I thought you didn't believe in love?" Kathy challenged testily.

"I don't, but you do," he reminded her. "So let her work it out whatever way she thinks is best."

"I don't have any other choice, do I?"

"Hey. You didn't want to fight about anything, remember?"

She sighed impatiently. "Then you could agree with me when I'm upset and worried about her."

"She's a smart woman," he said quietly. "She's nobody's victim. She must have faith in this guy for reasons you don't see. Anyway—it *is* generous of you to dedicate your royalties to her."

"It's only money."

Gib had to agree with her. For someone who'd had only money for a major part of his life, he understood its intrinsic lack of significance in the space of a lifetime.

Chapter Six

"The Crescent City," Kathy said excitedly, peering through the shaded window of the limo driving her, her mother and Gib from the airport to their hotel in the French Quarter. "Home of General Pierre Beauregarde, Frances Parkinson Keyes, Louis Armstrong and pralines!"

"Forget the pralines," Patsy cautioned. "You have a wardrobe that has to fit you for three more weeks. Concentrate on the crayfish."

The small hotel was old and wonderful with a wrought iron balcony that looked out onto the street below. Pots of flowers filled the corners of the balcony and baskets spilling colorful flowers hung from overhead.

Bright sunlight bathed the street as Kathy leaned both hands on the railing and breathed in the sunny day. She heard the lyrical sounds of Southern voices and caught an aromatic whiff of a bakery, or some talented woman's kitchen.

Patsy peered over the railing with her, then yawned daintily. "It is beautiful, but I'm exhausted. Flights at 6:00 a.m. should be illegal."

"Mmm." Kathy heard the complaint but was unable to process it as anything that affected her. She was in New Orleans! It was only ten o'clock in the morning and she didn't have to be anywhere until the middle of the afternoon.

"I'm taking a nap," her mother announced, patting another delicate yawn. "You should rest a little, too."

"I'm going exploring," Kathy said, energized by the sunshine and the drama and history of the city below. "You take it easy. I'm going to track down that aroma and bring something back, but not until I've wandered around."

"Kathy, Gib's in the shower and I don't—"

That was all Kathy heard. She snatched her purse off the fainting couch near the balcony and blew her mother a kiss. "Don't worry, I'll be fine. I was fine before I had a bodyguard, and I'll be fine now. Rest well."

"Kathy, I don't..."

Kathy closed the door on her mother's objections and followed the narrow corridor to the carpeted stairs, then across an old lobby with claret carpets, Corinthian columns, Caribbean art on the walls and potted palms flanking the stained-glass doors.

She stepped out onto the sunny sidewalk, drew another deep breath and felt it all the way to her toes. Across the street a man sat on the sidewalk playing something torchy on a clarinet, his hat holding several green bills and a scattering of change that gleamed in the sunlight.

Kathy crossed the street, added a couple of bills to the hat, then turned west down the street.

GIB HURRIEDLY PULLED ON gray twill slacks and a light blue sweater as Patsy continued to shout at him through the bathroom door.

"I'm sure she's all right, but it is a strange city and I'm not sure I like the idea..." She went on but Gib tuned her out as he pulled on socks and shoes, already sure that he didn't like the idea, either.

And he was going to make that clear when he caught up with Kathy.

"What was she wearing?" he asked Patsy as he hurried past her to his room to collect his wallet and keys. The keys, he thought absently, opened absolutely nothing in New Orleans, but he pocketed them, anyway. They represented his stuff.

"She didn't change. Jeans and a red sweater."

Right. He remembered thinking, when they'd all walked down to the limo that morning in Orlando at the ungodly hour of 4:30 a.m., how fresh she'd looked for a woman who'd done nothing but rush from one appointment to another with only brief breaks in between.

And he remembered some sartorial advice he'd once overheard that redheads should never wear red, and yet she looked sensational, the sweater's deep, rich red somehow not at all at odds with her carroty hair. A filigreed silver clip had held it at the back of her neck, smooth bangs fringing her forehead.

A clarinetist on the sidewalk across from the hotel ended a piece on a long, bluesy note as Gib stepped out into the sun and looked up, then down the street, undecided which direction Kathy would have taken.

"Pretty redhead?" the musician asked with a grin. "Mind of her own?"

Gib smiled and walked toward him. "That's her."

The man pointed west. "That way."

"Thanks." Gib put a big bill in the man's hat.

"Thank *you.*"

According to the guidebook Gib had perused on the plane, this old section of New Orleans had no such thing as zoning, so taverns did a brisk business beside churches, and schools could be found near areas where another kind of business was also brisk but never talked about.

There was evidence of that problematic but interesting eclecticism in the couple of blocks Gib walked, in his search for Kathy. He looked into storefronts, and even into taverns, not putting it past her to check them out in her fascination with the city.

A virgin on the loose in the Vieux Carre. Great.

And then he spotted her half a block up and across the street, peering into a window. It was a bakery window, he saw as he drew closer. She ducked inside before he could reach her.

When she came out a couple of minutes later, biting into a doughnut, a white paper bag in her other hand, he caught her arm with more force than necessary to make a point.

She gasped in surprise and her doughnut went flying. She turned startled blue eyes on him, then choked as her indrawn breath caught the sugar that coated the doughnut.

Feeling instantly guilty, he slapped her back until she recovered. She finally looked up at him, eyes watery, cheeks pink. "Why did you do that?" she demanded.

"To get your attention," he snapped back at her, catching her arm again and reviving his annoyance with her. "What if I'd been some thief, or some jerk bent on taking up Morganstern's challenge?"

She tried to yank away from him but he held firm. "I'd knee you in the groin," she replied in a sharp but low voice. "You want me to demonstrate?"

"Don't get smart with me," he warned, barely resisting an impulse to shake her. "I'm on this tour for your protection."

"Then why," she asked coolly, "are you bruising me?"

He dropped his hand from her and closed his eyes. He'd have counted to ten but he was too exasperated to remember how.

"I want to find a bouquet of flowers," she said, her voice less angry though hardly penitent. "You can come with me if you lighten up."

She started off, but he caught her arm and pulled her back to him, determined to win this one. He knew threats wouldn't do it, so he resorted shamelessly to emotional blackmail.

"The security of three dear old ladies rests in your hands, Kathy," he said reasonably. "So far, they've put out an awful lot of money on you, and the only thing that's going to get that back for them is your book. If anything happened to you—"

"If anything happened to me," she interrupted, holding his gaze, "it'd be a bestseller for sure. But I know your aunts would be upset. So, fine. Keep tabs on me, but don't crowd me. You know how precious your space is to you. I've spent months of my spare time confined at home, writing, then revising the darn book, and I'm not going to spend my days in New Orleans in a hotel room! Lovely as it is."

"I wouldn't expect you to," he replied evenly, "but if you'd have given me ten minutes to finish my shower, I'd have happily escorted you." He started to walk, a firm grip on her arm. "Let's find flowers."

"You have to replace my doughnut first."

"God."

THEY SHARED a beignette and a cup of coffee as they walked slowly up and down the wonderful old streets. They found flowers at the French Market, an institution since before the turn of the nineteenth century. Gib bought her a fat bunch of roses of various colors.

"We're only going to be here two and a half days," he said, handing them to her.

She sniffed the wonderful fragrance and looked at him over the colorful blooms, failing to understand how that was a problem.

"What are you going to do with them when we leave?" he asked. "You can't take them on a flight out of the state."

"I'm going to enjoy them for two and a half days," she replied. "Then I'll leave them for the woman who cleans the room."

"There are flowers all over our patio."

She nodded. "Those belong to the hotel. These are mine." She sniffed them again and sighed her approval.

He put an arm around her shoulders and drew her along with him. "Possessive little devil, aren't you?"

She opened her eyes and looked into his. "Is that what frightens you about me?"

He looked puzzled. "You don't frighten me. Except when you run off into a strange city by yourself."

She tucked the bakery bag into her purse and looped her free arm around his waist. "I'd challenge you on that, but it's much too beautiful a day to argue."

"There are good and bad weather conditions for arguments?"

"I don't know. I haven't had that many arguments. Except with my mother, and those don't count because she sounds as though she's making sense but she really isn't. I can never keep up with her, and eventually I lose by default."

They walked all over the French Quarter, had lunch at Henri's on Canal Street, visited the Presbytère, an old court chambers that now functioned as a museum of Louisiana artifacts.

They went on to visit several historic homes, then rode back to the hotel in a horse-drawn carriage.

Kathy leaned into Gib's shoulder. "This is the best day I've had since..." She paused to think, then finished in some surprise, "This is the best day I've *ever* had."

"That's a pretty extravagant statement, considering you were forced to allow your bodyguard along."

She giggled. "But you had the money for the carriage ride home, so it all worked out."

He barked a laugh and playfully tightened the arm around her neck.

KATHY'S VISIT to a radio talk-show went well, with a fairly equal number of supporters and detractors calling in. The detractors were more disbelieving than scornful, so she felt the evening was better than a draw.

The following day she appeared on an afternoon talk-show with a host and hostess who had invited the local chairman of a mothers' group whose cause was to slow down and eventually eradicate teenage pregnancy. Also on the panel was a televangelist whose position was more judgmental than spiritual.

Kathy was beginning to regret her appearance on the show when he said in an oratorical voice, "We gotta stop these kids from sinnin' and ruinin' our welfare programs and their babies' lives."

"Their love isn't a sin," Kathy said calmly, wondering what would happen to her sales if she punched him in the nose on statewide television. "Some of them don't get love at home and hope to find it in sexual relationships and with babies of their own. But that all falls apart when they face the reality of emotionally supporting each other and materially supporting a baby. I don't think we should call them sinners, they're just young and unaware of their choices."

The mother jumped in to support Kathy, and the rest of the program was a verbal battle among the three of them. When Kathy finally unclipped her microphone at the end of the show, she felt as though she'd failed her whole purpose in being on the program.

The hostess, Bridget Marshall, was a beautiful brunette with a friendly manner. She hooked an arm in Kathy's. "Why don't I take you to a jazz club tonight? You haven't really seen New Orleans unless you've listened to Jazz on Bourbon Street."

Kathy had to agree. Her mother had talked about having dinner at Antoine's, but this had more appeal.

Bridget handed Kathy her business card. "I'll pick you up at eight."

GIB WAS NOT PLEASED with her plans.

"Did you hear anything I said this morning?" he demanded.

They stood together in the small living room where Kathy was rearranging the roses she'd placed in a vase that afternoon. She was dressed and waiting for Bridget.

Gib wore a graphite-colored Cerruti suit and a white shirt. "I heard everything you said," Kathy replied. She removed the bud off the stem of a white rose and tucked it into the lapel of Gib's jacket. "I couldn't very well turn down a TV personality, could I, when this tour is all about favorable publicity?"

Patsy wandered out of her bedroom adjusting a pearl earring. "I think Gib's right," she said. "A jazz club sounds like fun, but the potential for—"

A knock on the door announced Bridget's arrival. Kathy made introductions, then left with Bridget.

Gib picked up the silky black wrap Patsy had dropped on the back of the sofa and placed it over her shoulders. "Minor change in plans," he said. "Do they serve dinner at jazz clubs?"

"Got me."

"We're about to find out."

"But *which* jazz club? She didn't say."

"Bridget mentioned Bobby Charles. I saw a marquee with his name on it while Kathy and I were out today."

Patsy patted his arm. ''A detective as well as a bodyguard. You should ask for more money.''

He laughed mirthlessly. ''I'm beginning to think there isn't enough money in this world to pay me for this tour.''

THE MUSIC was like nothing Kathy had ever heard. She didn't like the hot jazz, the endless riffs that probably indicated genius but that she personally found unpleasant to the ear.

But she loved the blues. Notes wept over each other up and down the scale, telling sad, sad stories without words. She was completely lost in such a number when Bridget said in pleased surprise, ''Oh, look! Danny!''

A handsome young man with dark hair and eyes approached their table. Bridget rose and was taken into his arms. ''When did you get back?'' she asked him as he kissed her cheek. ''It's been ages! What are you doing these days?''

''I've been in D.C.,'' he replied, his voice fading as he noticed Kathy. ''I'm back for a-an interview with...'' He laughed over his sudden inability to concentrate. ''Sorry. I forgot what I'm doing here. Who are you?''

Kathy laughed and held up her hand. ''Kathryn McQuade. Hi.''

Bridget sat and pulled him down into the seat between her and Kathy. ''This is Daniel Brussard. He and I started out together as go-fors for the station. He plays mean tennis, loves whitewater rafting and has a very dangerous line of flattery, so watch yourself. Kathy was on the show today, Danny. She's written a book about virginity.''

Danny pretended to shake. "Virginity? They're not bringing it back are they?"

"She's trying to. Oh, damn! There's my beeper." Bridget stood. "You guys chat while I run into the ladies' room with my cell phone and see who's disturbing my dinner and why."

The waiter came and Danny ordered bourbon. Kathy watched him, thinking how New Orleans it all was—a handsome man with a French surname ordering bourbon in a smoky jazz club.

Kathy declined a refill on her wine, and the waiter disappeared.

Danny leaned toward her. "You are the prettiest thing to cross my path in years," he said with a charm she recognized as carefully polished. It simply added to the atmosphere. "What's this about virginity?"

"It's a personal philosophy," she replied, "but there's a lot more to me than that. I—"

"How old are you?" he interrupted.

"Twenty-six."

"And you've never...?"

"No."

His brown eyes widened in disbelief. "A pretty thing like you? Where do you come from, and what's wrong with the men there?"

Kathy kept smiling. She came up against this attitude all the time. "Sex should happen as a result of a meeting of souls, a commitment of hearts. It shouldn't matter how pretty you are, or how old you are. If you're forty and haven't found someone you can truly love, I don't think you should give yourself away."

"Give yourself away." He repeated her words

slowly, carefully, narrowing his focus on her as though decoding some message there. His eyes suddenly widened again as though he'd been enlightened. "Of course. You mean you want a man who'll share with you."

She nodded. "Of course. Every woman wants that."

He took her hand, held it between his two and smiled wolfishly. "I'm him."

Kathy was thinking he wasn't quite as interesting as she'd originally imagined, but he had to have feelings, too, so she smiled politely as she withdrew her hand.

"Why is that?" she asked.

"Yearly salary in the middle six figures," he replied. "Stock portfolio, apartments in Paris and Manhattan..."

She was wondering how that related to his being a giving man, when he clarified it for her.

"I can give you whatever you want." He looked over that part of her visible above the table as though to suggest her needs were obviously simple. "A piece of jewelry, the lease on a new Beamer. Or—let's face it—nothing's quite as satisfying as good old cash."

Kathy stared at him a moment, fighting a desperate need to laugh. Her magical and atmospheric evening had suddenly taken on a comic quality.

"Danny," she said, wondering if there was even any point in trying to explain, "I meant a man who'll give of him*self,* who'll share his thoughts and his feelings."

She could tell when he gave her the wolfish smile again that she hadn't gotten through to him. "Come on," he coaxed, reaching for her hand a second time. "You're telling me you wouldn't go to bed with a man who made it worth your while?"

"That's what I'm telling you."

"Even if he had untapped depths of charm?"

GIB WAS BEGINNING to feel like some dimestore James Bond. He and Patsy were seated at a small round table across the room from Kathy and Bridget and the Armani suit ad that just joined table.

Ordinarily Gib wouldn't have cared if Kathy had spotted him, but strange things seemed to be happening around her so he watched the action behind the partial concealment of a tall coachlike lamp in the middle of the minuscule table.

"What is going on?" Patsy asked in puzzlement.

"Not sure," Gib replied. Bridget had just left Kathy at the table with the new arrival and had hurried toward the ladies' room while pulling her cell phone out of her purse.

But the moment she'd cleared the club's main room, she'd reached for a bag on top of a coatrack in the hallway that led to the rest rooms. The fortuitous location of Gib's and Patsy's table allowed Gib a fairly clear view of her actions.

"I think," he said quietly to Patsy as he watched Bridget pull a camera out of the bag, "that we've happened upon a setup. No, don't turn around. The chummy reporter had a camera stashed in the hallway."

"You're kidding!"

"Nope. She's focusing on the table right now."

The man had Kathy's hand and was apparently reeling out some kind of line to which she seemed receptive. Gib felt angry, disappointed and eager for a fight—emotions usually foreign to him.

Normally he considered anger destructive and debilitating and seldom succumbed to it, but something different was fueling it this time. Something dark and elemental that didn't allow his customarily reasonable approach to take over.

He wasn't normally one to be disappointed in people, because his childhood had taught him not to expect much from them. But he found himself very disappointed that Kathy seemed to consider the designer ad appealing.

And he could count on three fingers the times he'd ever come to blows with anyone, and all those times had been before high school. Once he'd learned to employ reason, and also learned not to expect much, there'd been very few reasons to want to brawl about anything.

Until now.

Until Kathy.

As he watched her, she pulled her hand out of the man's grasp and reached for her purse.

The man stood and caught her arm and said something that caused a tightening of her expression. She responded with something quick and angry and a toss of her head that appeared to be some final punctuation.

He put his arms around her, clearly trying to coax and cajole her.

In the hallway, Bridget had leaned around the door frame and was focusing on them.

Gib started for the table, instinct sending him to protect Kathy's physical safety. But he veered off toward the hallway, thinking that she had told him that morning that she had an effective if primitive self-defense strategy, and all she'd worked for was in jeopardy if photos of her in a clinch in a jazz bar ever got to the tabloids or the ten o'clock news as was clearly Bridget's intention.

But Patsy pushed him in Kathy's direction. "I'll get the reporter, you go to Kathy."

Gib had taken two steps when he heard a slap, a shout and the sound of breaking glass. Everyone in the club rose to their feet to see what was happening, and he was forced to push his way through them, fear for Kathy now uppermost in his mind.

He shouldn't have hesitated, he told himself. He shouldn't have given her reputation and her career a second thought when her body was in jeopardy.

Gib cleared the throng just in time to catch the designer ad as he reeled backward into him with a high-pitched wail, both hands gripping the spot Kathy knew to be a man's Achilles'—well.

Kathy dusted off her hands, slapped her purse on a nearby empty table and leaned over the semiconscious man hanging from Gib's arms. "I said no," she told him mildly.

The women in the room squealed and applauded.

Kathy focused on Gib in surprise. "Hi. What are you doing here?"

Momentarily off balance because of her apparent calm, he indicated the man he still supported. "Let me get rid of this guy and I'll explain."

Gib dragged him out a side door and sat him down next to a lineup of garbage cans in the alley, appreciating the poetic justice of the gesture.

Back inside the club, everyone was seated once again, and the musicians were preparing to pick up where Kathy had interrupted them. Kathy, however, was nowhere in sight.

A big man on the base pointed Gib toward the hallway. "Some lady shouted her name."

Gib did find Kathy in the hallway, arguing with her mother, who was seated astride Bridget's prone body, yanking the film cartridge out of her camera.

A small, nervous-looking man who introduced himself to Gib as the club's manager, told him he'd called the police.

"Mother, let her *up!*" Kathy was saying, trying to pull her mother to her feet.

"I think a few words to the right people about what you do in your spare time," Patsy said, ignoring Kathy as Bridget, enraged and helpless, screamed and squirmed under her, "would certainly make for an interesting story."

"What are you talking about?" Kathy demanded.

Gib explained about Bridget hiding in the hallway and photographing her and the man obviously hired to try to make her change her mind about sex.

"You can't be serious?" Kathy looked down at Bridget in horror. "That's why you invited me here? To set me up and get a better, juicier story?"

Bridget, incoherent in her rage, screamed and turned her face away. "Let me up!" she demanded.

Gib reached into the open bag on the floor beside her and pulled out a new film cartridge. He took the now empty camera from Patsy, inserted the cartridge, closed the back of the camera and turned the winder until the film was in position.

Then he took several steps back, far enough to allow him to frame Bridget with Patsy astride her in the viewfinder and focused.

"Smile," he said.

Patsy smiled. Bridget screamed. Gib took half a dozen shots. Then he advanced the film until it was completely wound and removed it from the camera. He pocketed the cartridge and replaced the camera in Bridget's bag and squatted down beside her still-prone body.

"If you're tempted to create a story out of what you tried to make happen here tonight—either for your station or any one of the sleazy tabs that might be interested in this kind of thing—" he patted his pocket that contained the cartridge "—remember that I have this, and I promise you I'm far more ruthless than you ever thought of being."

The police arrived a moment later. Bridget, now on her feet and very rumpled, was recognized by one of the officers.

"Miss Marshall," he said, unabashedly starstruck. Then he frowned at her appearance. "What happened?"

She opened her mouth and pointed to Gib and Patsy, as though prepared to accuse them of manhandling. But Gib patted his pocket again, and she changed her mind.

"It was just a misunderstanding, Officer," she said, gathering up her things.

The officer turned to the manager. "Is that true, René?"

René nodded quickly. "I saw the ruckus and wasn't sure what had happened, so I called you. Seems it was simply a—" he glanced at Gib, who nodded "—a friendly disagreement."

The officer frowned at Bridget's disheveled appearance. "Friendly?"

"Friendly," she repeated with a false smile.

The policeman finally accepted the explanation and left. Bridget snatched up her bag and left, too, without another word.

In the main room, the small band was at work again, a heartbreaking melody coming from a trumpet solo.

Gib smiled down at Kathy. "So. We're dealing with a warrior virgin."

She sighed a little sadly. So much for her real New Orleans evening. Bridget's offer of friendship and support had been phony and malicious. "The term *virgin* is not synonymous with *defenseless simpleton.*"

"You've made that clear. You want to go home?"

She did. She felt hurt and betrayed and terribly stupid. She wanted nothing more than to go back to their hotel room and hide under the blankets.

Deep down, she even found the idea of going home—home to Bayside—very appealing. Sustaining an unpopular position was growing wearisome.

But she remembered the faces of the young people at St. Joan of Arc High School. And she remembered her mother's debts.

"No," she said finally. "Let's stay for a while. You want to dance?"

Gib looked surprised.

"Virgins dance, you know," she said with mild impatience.

"I know," he replied. "Bodyguards just don't do it that much."

She folded her arms and studied him with grim acceptance. "Speaking of bodyguards, you followed me here on instinct?"

He met her gaze without flinching. "Good thing, wasn't it?"

"Yes," she admitted grudgingly. "It was."

He took her hand and led her onto the small dance floor.

Chapter Seven

Dancing with Gib was torture because being held by him was wonderful. He may not have considered himself a good dancer, but Kathy thought him very skilled at standing in a very small space and swaying to the music—which was all there was room to do on the small floor, anyway.

One of his hands held her between the shoulder-blades, and the other at the small of her back.

She wrapped both arms around his neck, keeping her eyes averted to the smoky room, doing her best to appear as relaxed and unmoved by their closeness as he seemed to be.

It was ironic, she thought, as she fought the need to turn her mouth to his and see if he would respond, that Bridget had attempted to stage a scene that might have played out on its own if she'd simply waited. But with Gib instead of Danny.

Not that a kiss in itself was injurious to a virgin's reputation, but she felt sure Bridget could have reported it with enough implication to make it more than it was.

Not that it *was* going to be at all. Patsy, dancing with the club's manager, was getting more interest out of a complete stranger than Kathy was getting out of the man with whom she'd been virtually joined at the hip for the past week and a half.

"*Now* are you ready to go?" Gib asked.

Kathy sighed and leaned back a little to look into his eyes. She was conscious of his hands moving together to hold her close enough to protect her from the couple behind them.

"You're not enjoying this at all, are you?" she asked.

Gib looked over the crowd, then back at her, and she caught a glimpse of something deep and powerful in his eyes. It was so strong that she was amazed nothing else about him betrayed it.

Her lips parted as she suspected what it was, what it meant.

"It's late" he said, finally reaching up to gently pull her arms from around his neck. "You have a press conference at ten in the morning."

She let him get away with that until they reached the hotel. As usual, her mother collapsed the moment the action stopped and went right to bed like a caged bird over whom someone had dropped a cover.

Gib went into the small kitchen to make his nightly pot of coffee. This one was the chicory blend for which the South was famous.

Kathy knelt on the sofa and leaned her elbows on the back of it, watching him at work in the small alcove fitted with stove, microwave and very small refrigerator.

"Do you like that chicory stuff?" she asked. He'd ignored her all the way home in the limousine, and she was determined to talk about what had happened tonight.

"It's all right," he replied, fitting the coffee basket in place. "Better than that hazelnut stuff. You're going to have bags under your eyes in the morning."

"So are you."

That made him turn to her in puzzlement, precisely what she'd wanted. Yes. That look remained in his eyes. He'd tried to cover it with casual unconcern as he went about his nightly ritual, but she saw it. She liked to think it came out to meet her.

He raised an eyebrow in question.

"You're not going to be able to sleep," she explained, crossing her arms on the back of the sofa. "You discovered tonight that you care about a woman you haven't slept with."

He turned on the pot with an impatient jab of the button, then remained where he was, one hand on the counter, the other in his pocket as he regarded her with a frown. "That was sexual interest," he said, a little brutally, she thought. "Not love."

"Oh, I know it wasn't love." She smiled, knowing he expected her to be hurt. "But it was more than sexual interest. It was the discovery that you may have encountered a woman you'd want more than sex from."

"I think you're putting a fairy-tale spin on what was just a seductive moment on the dance floor."

"Seductive." She savored the word, certain it was proof of her point. "That implies that the seductee has been attracted and charmed. Those qualities have holding power."

"Not for me," he insisted quietly.

Kathy got to her feet and walked around the sofa

to confront him without touching him, though she was close enough if either of them reached out. "So, you're not going to admit that you're beginning to feel something for me?"

He smiled fractionally. "Does exasperation count?"

"You know what I mean," she scolded softly.

"No," he said, "I don't. Because I've never experienced it."

She studied him long and hard, but he'd had time to collect himself and had managed to conceal what she'd seen.

She smiled and reached up to kiss his cheek. "Well, watch yourself, London. You're going to."

NEITHER KATHY NOR GIB slept well, and they awoke with barely half an hour to prepare for the press conference. Patsy was still asleep.

Kathy showered in five minutes, hurriedly applied makeup, expediently knotted her hair into a fashionably untidy bun and pulled on a baggy, but elegant, lavender linen suit.

Gib chased her to the elevator while slipping into a brown tweed sports jacket over brown slacks and a beige T-shirt.

Light burst in their faces the instant the elevator doors opened in the lobby.

"Whoa! Gentlemen!" Gib moved in front of Kathy and pushed the crowd back.

Someone shoved the morning newspaper into Kathy's hands. "What do you have to say, Miss McQuade?"

Kathy felt strobe lights going off around her as she focused on the front-page photo of Danny Brussard dangling from Gib's hands just before Gib had dragged him outside. Kathy stood opposite, knee still bent. The caption read, "Soldier Virgin Repels Unwanted Advance."

Kathy was sufficiently aware of her surroundings to have full control of her expression. She looked up with a smile at the sea of faces. "This really isn't news, ladies and gentlemen. Women have been coping with such aggressive advances since time began and warding them off in the same way."

"Check the photo below the fold," someone shouted.

Kathy flipped the paper—and had difficulty biting back the gasp that rose to her lips. There, six columns wide, was a photo of her and Gib on the dance floor. It had been taken at the moment when she'd leaned back in his arms to look into his eyes.

She'd just suggested that he wasn't enjoying dancing with her at all, and he'd met her gaze, revealing quite the opposite, though he'd denied it all evening.

And that was clearly visible in the photograph. His eyes were turbulent, his brow furrowed, his jaw tight. The photo had been taken at Kathy's back so that his clasped hands were visible just below her shoulderblades. The ends of her hair lapped against his knuckles, and he'd unconsciously caught a curly strand between the first and second fingers of his right hand.

He looked like a man at the mercy of the moment—and the woman in his arms.

Yes! Kathy thought triumphantly. *Tell me you aren't interested, Gib London.*

Then a reporter asked, "You falling under the virgin's spell, Mr. London? It's all over town that

Bridget Marshall tried to set up Miss McQuade, but that photo taken afterward makes me wonder if she shouldn't have just waited and let nature take its course. The two of you look pretty...involved."

Someone had handed Gib a paper, too, and he looked up from it and into Kathy's eyes. For an instant he wore the same look he wore in the photo—as though he was angry at Kathy for something he seemed to consider all her fault.

Then he handed the paper back to the nearest reporter, reached out for Kathy's hand and took her with him to the podium already set up with microphones.

Kathy went obligingly, wondering herself what was about to happen.

"If you've read your publicity packets," he said, taking the lead while Kathy stood beside him, "you know that I'm Gib London, financial officer of London Publishing, and nephew of the current publishers. My aunts asked me to accompany Miss McQuade on tour because of Howard Morganstern's challenge that the young men of America try to change her mind about sex, on the chance that someone might become overly enthusiastic in accepting the challenge."

"You the same Gilbert London who earned one of the three Medals of Honor given in Somalia?" was shouted from the back of the audience.

"I am. But this tour is about Miss McQuade."

The same voice insisted, "That photo looks as though it's about Miss McQuade and *you*."

Kathy awaited his answer, caught somewhere between concern for what this would do to the tour and ultimately the sales of her book, and what it would do for their relationship if he would admit that he *was* beginning to feel something for her.

To her complete surprise, he looked out at the reporters with a guilty but unembarrassed smile. It was a definitively masculine admission of sexual vulnerability.

The men in the group laughed, the women smiled at one another and shook their heads.

"One of you suggested earlier that Bridget Marshall could have saved herself a lot of trouble if she'd just let 'nature take its course,'" he said, "but if you haven't read Kathy's book, you don't realize that she isn't opposed to nature doing its work, but insists that your brain should operate before your body does." Now he smiled apologetically. "So, if you're wondering if something happened between us last night, I assure you nothing did. And nothing will."

"You mean you agree with her?" a reporter asked in astonishment. Laughter filled the room.

Gib laughed, too. "No, but I'm the financial officer of the publishing house that published her book. It's in my best interest to see that she holds firm."

A young female reporter took a step out of the crowd and raised her pen to catch Gib's attention. "Financially, it would be." She held up the bottom half of the front page. "But what about your personal interests?"

"They don't matter for the length of this tour," he insisted politely. "My job is to look out for her personal interests. Now. You've heard enough from me. Kathy?"

Gib extended a hand to her, held it until she stood in place behind the microphones, then stepped aside.

She had no idea what she said. Her mind was filled with the memory of that look he'd given the reporters—and the fact that whatever he felt seemed to mean nothing to him.

Her brain on automatic setting, she answered questions, accepted their jokes goodnaturedly and made a few of her own. Then the press conference was over and she and Gib and her mother hurried upstairs to pack in order to reach the airport for their three o'clock flight.

"THIS OUGHT to make you happy," Gib said, pointing through the wall of glass that separated the terminal's waiting area from the plane whose belly was being stuffed with luggage.

Kathy, who'd been distracted all morning, looked up from a magazine she wasn't reading. "Why?"

Gib pointed again. "Jets."

She forced a smile. "Oh. Right." Then went back to her magazine.

Her life, she'd decided during that morning's press conference, was powered by propellers, not jets. Gib claimed that propellers were dependable and allowed landings at smaller airports—qualities he apparently considered a plus.

But as a metaphor for the direction her life was taking, she didn't think it was. Dependable. Suitable for small destinations. That pretty much described her.

But she'd wanted bigger things for herself. Best-selling mystery novels and the love of an exciting man.

And what did she have? A book on virginity and an exasperatingly private man who'd just told a room filled with reporters that she could never mean anything to him.

A couple of days ago she might have been able to accept that with equanimity.

But today she was in love.

It had happened the moment he looked out at the news crews and gave them that smile that admitted she'd touched him. It was the only time since she'd met him—except for last night on the dance floor—that she'd seen any suggestion of vulnerability in him.

She'd been deliriously happy for about a minute, then he'd become once again the man she was more familiar with—the man who refused to be affected by what he felt.

And that was the man with whom she had to spend the next two and a half weeks.

She hoped that thought didn't make her look as pinched and irascible as it made her feel. If so, she would look like everyone's idea of a virgin and undermine her own cause.

They were on the plane, carry-ons stowed overhead, her purse under her feet, seat belt fastened, her mother seated between her and Gib, when Kathy realized that she had to take positive action against becoming her own worst enemy.

This book was going to free her mother from debt—at least some of it—and set Kathy up to sell a clever mystery series featuring a female insurance investigator.

Who needed a man for that? Who needed a man for anything? She'd lived without sex this long. How hard could it be to keep going without it?

She felt a little dip in her positive surge at the

realization that it *would* be harder now. She'd often wondered what the experience would be like, imagined herself in bed with one or two of the men she'd dated, but she'd never really *wanted* sex with anyone the way she suddenly wanted it with Gib. Because this was the dynamite combination she wanted all women to wait for—sex with the man you love.

Unfortunately her theory made no provision for what to do if the man didn't love you.

She sighed, closed her eyes and leaned her head back against the comfortable headrest. So what? Life was about learning to deal with what you had, because, as most people could attest, it was seldom what you wanted.

Her spirit was bigger than the problem. She would be fine. Without Gib London.

THE FIVE DAYS in St. Louis and Minneapolis went by in a blur. Gib had hated every one of them. It had been rainy and cold, a weather pattern covering most of the central United States and their hotel room specifically.

It amazed him that Kathy could look perky and wonderful, speak politely, smile *all* the time, yet react to him like the icy heart of a blizzard whenever he approached her, without ever dropping the smile.

He ignored her on the chance that she was trying to force a confrontation. He didn't want to have to deal with what he felt for her or what was going on between them until he understood it, and he didn't think that was going to happen anytime soon.

He thought that generally her ideas were unnecessarily punitive and made little real sense.

Yet his mind was now filled with images of the

two of them in the middle of his bed. Every time this happened, he would turn to some other project, try to think about something else, but the insistent image would return and he would find himself embellishing it with detail.

He could see himself easing her nervousness by revering her body inch by silky inch, by initiating her with a tenderness that would take most of the night.

Then, when dawn broke and she was used to his touch, he would show her what could happen when all cautions and constraints were tossed to the wind and love was made with wild abandon.

He hadn't endured such torture since he'd been fourteen and attending Burgess-Tully, a private high school in the Florida Keys. His mother had been recovering from the breakup of a relationship that had taken place while she was between husbands two and three.

The headmaster had had a daughter who loved to sunbathe in the nude, and Gib and several of his classmates would watch her from an orange tree outside the chapel.

Thanks to Kathy McQuade, he'd forgotten the mature and slightly jaded lovemaking of his adulthood and remembered only the lusty yearnings of his adolescence.

It occurred to him that there was a sharp honesty that tied what he felt now to what he'd felt then, but experience reminded him that love wasn't about honesty, so he dismissed the thought.

The aunts called when Gib, Kathy and Patsy reached the hotel in Denver on the fourteenth day of the tour. Kathy was in the shower, and Patsy was napping.

"Darling," Rose said gently. Gib could hear the rustle of a newspaper somewhere in the background. "Is everything going...according to plan?"

"Yes," he replied with a heartiness he'd learned to fake to match Kathy's perpetual smile. "Everything's going beautifully. Kathy is eloquent and convincing and always prepared. Everyone seems to love her."

"Well. Dear. That's what we're worried about."

He knew precisely what she meant but pretended ignorance. "Worried about?" he asked innocently.

"Give me that!" he heard a familiar voice say forcefully. "Gilbert!" It was Cordelia. "I'm staring at a photo and article picked up by a wire service and credited to the *New Orleans Times Picayune.* The photo is of you and Kathy, her arms around your neck, your eyes devouring her. The caption suggests that you're the Bogey and Bacall of the next millennium." There was a very brief pause, but not long enough for him to say anything. "Now, correct me if I'm wrong, but aren't you supposed to be protecting our little virgin from harm rather than becoming a threat to her yourself?"

"Bogart and Bacall?" he repeated in disbelief.

"Famous for looks that said everything, for a chemistry that had no need of words." Paper rustled again, and there was a sharper sound, as though she'd slapped the paper onto a table. "Gib, what's happening?"

"Nothing," he assured her quickly, though deep in his heart he knew that to be a lie. But he wouldn't *let* it happen, and that was a truth his aunt could take to the bank. "That photo was taken after Kathy was befriended by a talk-show host, then set up to make it look as though she was falling for some Romeo's seduction."

"The paper says you knocked him out." That was Lucinda's voice, sounding thrilled by that possibility. He imagined all three aunts crowded around the phone in Cordelia's office. He'd never been able to convince her of the advantages of a speaker phone.

"No, Kathy knocked him out," he corrected. "I just arrived in time to catch him."

"Well, where were you?" That was Cordelia.

"I am on the job, Aunt," he assured her. "But Kathy's a little prickly about having me around all the time, so sometimes I have to keep my distance. It's also sometimes difficult to explain our cohabiting a hotel suite."

"But her mother's along! And all the suites have three bedrooms!"

"Aunt Cordie, you know the public. They'd much rather believe we're fooling around when no one's looking."

"It says here that you assured the press you aren't intimate."

"Do I even have to verify that for you?"

He heard urgent whispers and a low, unladylike growl. "No, you don't. But please be careful. Not only the future of this firm is at stake, but Patsy's financial future, and Kathy's reputation—as a writer and a woman."

Good. Why didn't they make him responsible for peace in the Middle East and a solution to world hunger while they were at it?

He assured them that he had all their best interests at heart and said his goodbyes.

He spotted the evening paper folded in three on the suite's simple oak slab coffee table and opened it cautiously.

He felt great relief when a photo of Hillary Clinton welcoming guests at a White House dinner occupied the front page. He was becoming convinced that even Kathy's advance publicity had missed the paper when he discovered the now-famous photo of him and Kathy on the front page of the entertainment section. Accompanying it was the same news story Cordelia had talked about, comparing him and Kathy to Bogart and Bacall.

He stared at it in dismay. What were they talking about? He had none of the craggy film star's dangerous looks, and Kathy's air was far more innocent than sultry.

But, he had to admit to himself as he stopped and stared at the photo, there was something in his eyes suggesting that despite the bricklike line of his jaw, he was lost to her.

He tossed the paper down again and went to the kitchen to check out the coffee supplies. He was trying to decide whether to go with the Colombian roast he needed, or the raspberry chocolate flavor Kathy was bound to prefer when he heard her scream.

And it wasn't just a scream, it was his name shrieked at the top of her voice.

He made it to her bedroom in seconds to find her holding two anxious-looking young boys at bay with a cordless curling iron. She wore only a towel, and her wet hair hung in dark strands past her shoulders.

Gib guessed the boys to be in their early teens, one of them tall and lanky in jeans and a Summit High sweatshirt and a baseball cap on backward. The other was shorter, thicker, and wore a football shirt with the name Boradino on the back, and the number twenty-six. Both were wide-eyed with panic.

"Hey, man, I'm sorry," the taller one said as Gib walked into the room. His frightened gaze went from an angry and shivering Kathy, then back to Gib. "We didn't mean anything, honest. We were all watching Morgenstern's show and talking about how great it would be to..." He swallowed audibly. "You know...do it with Kathy McQuade."

As Gib's jaw squared, the boy talked faster.

"No! That's not why we came! The guys dared us to get into the room, but we weren't going to...like...hurt her or anything."

"Yeah!" the other put in anxiously. "We were gonna be out of here before you got in, but these people were talking in the hallway and we couldn't get out without being seen, then we heard you coming and...and..."

"We hid in the closet," the tall one finished, swallowing noisily. "It was just a...dare. All the kids are talking about the book in life problems class."

Gib folded his arms and stood in the doorway. "How'd you get in?" he demanded.

"We sneaked in when the maid was cleaning the bathroom," Boradino said weakly. "And hid behind the sofa. When she left we went into the bedroom."

The tall one produced the slip the maid left for every guest with her name and the room number on it. "We had to bring this back," he said, handing it to Gib, then withdrawing his hand as though he feared losing it. "To prove that we got in."

"Elaborate scheme," Gib said, looking them over slowly. "It didn't occur to you that you'd frighten her to death, Boradino?"

"She wasn't supposed to find us!" he replied, his face paling. "We were supposed to be outta here… hey." Surprise that Gib had used his name finally registered on him.

The tall one backhanded him in the gut. "Dufus. Your name's on your shirt."

Boradino went crimson and closed his eyes in despair. "Maaan!" he whined.

"You read the book?" Gib looked at one boy, then the other.

They shook their heads.

"Okay." Gib leaned a shoulder in the doorway. "This can go one of two ways. I can hold you here while I call the desk and tell them I've caught two intruders."

"I vote we go the other way," the tall one put in quickly, then added on a sheepish note, "whatever that is."

Gib nodded. "Good. Number two it is. The two of you have to read Kathy's book and give a joint report to your life problems class. At Summit High, right?"

"Yeah. How'd you—" The tall one began to ask, then Boradino backhanded him and pointed to the front of his sweatshirt.

"Dufus yourself," Boradino said.

"What's your name?" Gib asked the other boy.

"Justin Miller," the boy replied.

"Okay. I guess we can assume you're going to

keep your part of the bargain here, since we know your names and where to find you.'' Gib hesitated a moment. They nodded. ''Good. And I guess we can also assume that you're not planning on lives of crime, because you really don't seem to have what it takes.''

The boys looked at each other in humiliation.

''But that's a good thing,'' Gib said. ''I like knowing you were basically too honest to conceal your identities.''

The boys shoulders squared just a little. Gib stepped out of the doorway. ''Get out of here.''

They stopped long enough to apologize to Kathy, then to thank Gib. Then they were gone, almost knocking over Patsy, who stepped hastily out of their way, glaring at them all the while. She followed them to the door.

Kathy was now shaking uncontrollably. Gib pushed her partially open closet door all the way and found her robe on the floor where she'd probably dropped it when she'd discovered them.

He snatched it up and wrapped it around her shoulders. ''There. You all right?''

She nodded, but he knew she lied because her shoulders and arms were stiff, and she still held the curling iron in front of her like a weapon.

He held the robe around her with one arm, then forced the curling iron from her with his other hand, turned it off and put it on the edge of the dresser.

Both her hands came up to clutch the arm he held around her. Her face crumpled. ''I don't... understand,'' she said in a high, horrified voice as she struggled to hold back tears. ''In New Orleans, I handled Danny Brussard without a second thought. But here..." She shook her head, her fingernails biting into his arm.

He wrapped the other arm around her, too, and held tightly. "You were prepared for Danny Brussard," he said gently. "These guys—though I don't think they meant you any real harm—took you by surprise and scared you. Virgins are allowed to be scared, aren't they?"

"I'm supposed to be...invincible."

"Who said?"

"I did."

Gib felt a tear fall onto his arm.

"A lot of...guys...are put off by what I think, and I've never had a father around, so I've pretty much had to...look out for Mom and me."

"Oh, you have not!" Patsy returned to the room, her movements fluttery as she tightened her own robe and moved around her daughter in concern. "You just take on too much—you always have. And then you wear yourself out and scare yourself to death."

Gib guessed Patsy's reaction was the result of concern for her daughter, but he frowned at her, anyway. "Maybe you could comfort her instead of scolding her?"

Patsy blinked at him, then studied her daughter leaning back into his embrace and gave him a sudden smile. Then she turned toward the door. "You seem to be doing all right. I'll put on the kettle."

Gib had a very wet head tucked into the hollow of his throat, and fingernails perforating his left forearm. The body in his arms was wrapped in terry cloth that obliterated its curves.

There was no reason he should feel aroused.

And yet he did.

Chapter Eight

Kathy closed her eyes and for several blissful moments just let herself feel.

The panic was beginning to abate, but her body still trembled involuntarily. At first that had alarmed her almost as much as finding two young men in her closet. Then Gib had wrapped an arm around her, and his grip was so strong she felt as though he had control of the situation.

That she liked the feeling surprised her. She'd always been so practical, eager to take on responsibility, willing to shoulder burdens. She was a leader by nature.

The manless life she'd led had exaggerated that in her, she knew, and she'd been sure that one day she would love a man, but would never really need one.

Now as she leaned her body back against Gib's and rested her head on his nicely rounded biceps, she realized with surprise that she'd turned over the moment to him and was basking in the pleasure of his protection.

Once she stopped shaking, surely she'd feel differently, but for now it was wonderful to be responsible for nothing at all.

His arms around her were tight, his cheek against hers warm and just a little rough, his body curved around hers had a possessive quality she was probably imagining but enjoyed, anyway.

Her trembling stopped, her internal controls kicked on again, and she felt her world right itself. But she felt no inclination to move.

She was herself again, and while she was perfectly willing to resume all her tasks and responsibilities, she realized with startling clarity that she could do everything without him, but she didn't want to.

He hadn't just relieved her of physical responsibility when he'd wrapped his arms around her, he'd shared her fear and her sense of inadequacy and had cut them in half. She felt as though that had doubled her strength.

But she still didn't want to move.

Well, she did, but it was only a slight turn of her head from his arm to his chin where she planted a light kiss. "Thank you," she whispered.

"You're welcome," he replied, kissing her forehead. And for one delicious moment he continued to hold her.

Then they heard the shrill whistle of the kettle and he dropped his arms from her. She couldn't help the smile on her lips when he turned her to face him.

He took one look at it and expelled an exasperated gasp. "How can you gloat when I was just trying to be helpful. You think the fact that I took you in my arms means I...?"

She stood on tiptoe and gave him another quick kiss to stop the flow of words. "I wasn't gloating," she corrected candidly. "Having your arms around me was so nice it made me smile. That's all."

He folded his arms and studied her doubtfully. "Really."

"Really. You shouldn't be so suspicious. You insist you feel nothing for me and I..." The smile threatened again, but she bit it back. "I think you believe that to be true."

His left eyebrow went up. "I *believe* that to be true?"

"Yes. Because you have so little experience with feelings. Positive ones." She patted his arm and tried to walk around him.

He caught hers and drew her back to him. "I warned you about invading my privacy."

She could no longer hold back the smile. "Now you're just looking for an excuse to kiss me."

Helpless frustration flared in his eyes, but she saw a grudging amusement there, too. "Neat trap," he said wryly. "You've got me coming or going."

She patted his cheek. "That's what love does to you." Then she walked around him and toward the kitchen in search of a cup of tea.

He was too astonished to stop her.

THE HOST on the Rocky Mountain Morning Show was a handsome, middle-aged man clearly intent on teasing Kathy. He showed the audience and the camera the wire service item picked up by the local paper about the fracas in New Orleans. He pointed a finger at the photo, then read the caption for the viewing audience.

"A smoldering Bogart and Bacall romance has come to Denver in the persons of Kathryn McQuade, author of *The Virgin Returns,* and Gib London, the handsome bodyguard hired by her publisher.'' The host looked into the camera and smiled. ''Bear with me while I read the first paragraph. 'The hot glances that warmed the Hollywood movie screens before graphic sex and bad language became a part of box office fare are back, and you'll never guess where. I noticed it first in New York where I went for an exclusive interview with...can't-say-who for now, then decided to fill a free afternoon by attending a press conference given by Kathy McQuade, *Virgin* authoress. I thought it would be good for a chuckle, but was surprised by the young woman's eloquence and sincerity.

'''I was also intrigued by the gorgeous man who is never more than three long-legged strides from McQuade. He has a Bogart presence, but a Kevin Costner face on a Tom Selleck frame. And his eyes are always on his charge, as is evident in the above photo. Lucky her. Would like to know what Massachusetts Representative Neil Barton thinks of all this.'''

The man folded the paper, put it aside and smiled companionably at Kathy seated on a small brocade couch. ''I guess what we're all wondering is how you hope to promote virginity when you're getting looks like that.''

The answer was easy. Not looking smug on local television because she loved seeing that photo was the hard part.

''Celibacy doesn't preclude attraction, romance or even lust,'' she answered. ''It just means you don't act upon them until the time is right.''

''You mean on the wedding night?''

"I mean when two thinking people have decided that they know each other well enough to share their most intimate selves—and can bear the consequences of what that means physically, emotionally, in every way. Logically, to me, that would make the parties want to commit to one another."

He frowned over that reply, then leaned toward her earnestly and asked, "Are you in love with Gib London, Kathy?"

Kathy, poise in place, parted her lips to give him a charming but evasive answer when she felt the blush rise at the neckline of her smoky blue sweater. She remembered how in books, a blush always "inched" its way up a heroine's face. In her case it whooshed up to her hairline as though she'd been dipped in fuchsia paint.

The host exclaimed and pointed to one of the cameramen, who did a closeup. The audience applauded. For the first time on the tour, Kathy was momentarily speechless.

Then she pulled herself together and raised her hands to quiet the audience. When their cheers and laughter were down to a low mumble, she said with dignity and a little self-deprecation, "Gib London's been a good friend and stalwart support to me on this tour," she said. "And I'm not used to having a man constantly beside me. I think I'm infatuated."

The host held up the photo. "I think he's beyond infatuated."

Trying to give Gib a break—at least with the hundreds of thousands of viewers watching—Kathy shook her head. "I think that photo's been misinterpreted. It's Gib's job to keep me safe, and I'd just punched out a masher and considerably upset our publicity plan. I think there's as much annoyance in that look as...well, whatever everyone's interpreting it to be."

As the audience laughed, the host announced the following day's guests and the credits began to roll.

Kathy concluded that that had been the longest fifteen minutes of her life.

THE ASPENS WERE GOLDEN, the oaks, red, the maples, copper. They flanked both sides of the narrow road and stretched on ahead as far as Kathy could see.

"How's this?" The limo driver, a big, middle-aged man with a pugilist's face and a grandmother's manner, peered at Kathy and Gib through the open shield that separated him from his passengers. "You want fall foliage, I found you fall foliage."

Kathy was delighted. The entire day, Sunday, was free, and her mother had opted to spend it in the hotel's spa.

But it was a cold, crisp fall day, and Kathy was desperate to remember what real life was like without hotel rooms and back-to-back appointments, and the press in pursuit of her every word and deed.

She turned eagerly to Gib. "Want to take a walk?"

"Sure." He pushed his door open, the simple word politely spoken but strangely uncommunicative. He'd been that way since yesterday afternoon.

But she refused to let his moodiness ruin her day.

"Do you mind waiting here for an hour, Sam?" she asked the driver. "Or, if you've got something else to do, you can come back for us."

Sam reached into the glove box and held up a

worn copy of a Robert Parker novel. "I can keep myself occupied for an hour, no problem. You two take your time. I'll be right here."

"Bless you, Sam. No, don't get out." Kathy followed Gib out of the limo, then started up the unpaved road. They were several miles out of Denver, and she could smell wood smoke, burning leaves and the indefinable perfume of fall.

She drew a deep breath and spread her arms out, embracing the morning. "Oh, Gib," she said, raising her face to the bright blue sky and drinking in the perfection of the day. "Did you ever smell anything so wonderful? Have you ever seen anything so beautiful? Have you ever felt so...perfect?"

He didn't want to answer that. He felt edgy and crotchety, but he didn't really want to rain on her parade, so to speak. She'd been a slave to their schedule without a single whine, and he knew she deserved this beautiful morning.

"Nice day," he finally forced himself to reply.

She undid the top button of a short, white sweater coat, then tossed the end of a bright pink scarf over her shoulder. She rolled her eyes at him. "'Nice day,'" she repeated in the same monotone he'd used. "If I were God, I'd hit you with a bolt of lightning for that understatement. He probably had to completely ignore the troubles in the former Soviet Union to create this sky and those trees and all you can say is 'Nice day'?"

"But I've spent two and a half weeks in your company," he replied with a grin. "I have special dispensation to be a little numb."

"Numb." She apparently didn't like that choice of words, either, but she tucked her arm in his and began to walk. Now attached to her, he was forced to follow. "How can you be alive on a day like this and claim to be numb?"

"Okay, that was an exaggeration."

"Relax," she encouraged with a squeeze of his arm. "Let yourself be happy."

He followed her down the narrow trail, trees aflame with color on both sides, and remembered a time when he'd always been relaxed. That is, he'd been somewhat driven to accomplish things, to succeed, but he'd always managed to enjoy his life. Until Kathy.

Now he found himself questioning everything and he didn't like it. He felt strangely discontented with what he had, what he wanted, what he thought.

Because all he thought about was her, all he wanted was her...all he *didn't* have was her.

He was neatly trapped in the quagmire of her virginity. If he'd wanted to explore the possibility that he felt something for her, he couldn't, because their innocent relationship was already compromised by that damned photo of him on the dance floor of that New Orleans jazz club. And everyone was now watching them.

That contributed considerably to his annoyance. He didn't like the fact that he had strangely complex feelings for Kathy "Virgin" McQuade, but he really didn't like that they showed on his face for all the world to see.

What had happened to him? He'd learned early to control every feeling so that it couldn't be trampled on or ignored by parents, stepparents, "uncles," "friends of the family." He'd thought he'd mastered the art of revealing nothing.

Yet, there it was on the front page of God-knew-how-many newspapers. The face of the tortured lover.

And it wasn't bad enough that he'd endured all that. Yesterday Kathy had reacted to that photo on television. When the interviewer had asked her if she was in love, Gib, off camera, had found himself holding on to the stand of an unused piece of camera equipment, waiting breathlessly for her answer.

Then she'd blushed furiously, and as the audience laughed and applauded, he'd felt his blood pressure go up a good ten points with unadulterated pleasure in that unprogrammed response.

Then she'd punctured his swollen ego with that so casual "I think I'm infatuated with him."

Infatuated. He was teetering on the brink of overthrowing everything experience had taught him, of abandoning a long-comfortable life-style, or actually giving serious thought to the possibility that he might be able to love someone. And she was "infatuated"?

He could have chewed granite.

They'd been walking half an hour, Kathy breathing in and breathing out like some turn-of-the-century patron of the Kellogg Health Club, when she said urgently, "What was that?"

Before he could ask what she'd seen or heard, she'd darted off into the trees.

"What? Kathy, wait!" He shouted after her, knowing even as he did that it wasn't going to stop her.

With a growl he ran into the gold and scarlet woods in pursuit of the bane of his existence.

He was an arm's length behind her when she

stopped without warning. He slammed into her, quickly raising his hands to protect her face and body as his forward momentum sent them into the sturdy trunk of an oak tree.

Kathy's startled cry rang in his ears as they collided with the rough bark. It bit into his knuckles and scraped his forehead.

Still, despite burning pain and annoyance over her sudden dash into the woods, Gib was sharply aware of every curve of her in his arms. Though the coat concealed them from view, he felt her breasts squashed against his ribs, one of her thighs forced between his, grazing his manhood, her round bottom filling one of the hands he'd used to try to protect her from the tree.

He was tough. He'd survived a loveless childhood, done two tours in Bosnia, kept order in a unit of strong and restless young men and intimidated a ruthless enemy.

But he'd suddenly had enough. He took hold of Kathy's shoulders and held her away from him, hoping that his body, if not his temper, would quiet down.

"What in the hell was that all about?" he demanded, his nerves frayed to rag.

She frowned and put a fingertip up to his forehead. "You're bleeding," she said in concern.

He yanked her hand away. "Of course I'm bleeding. Thanks to you I've just wrestled an oak tree! What were you doing?"

She pointed off to her right. "I heard..."

"We've had this discussion half a dozen times," he cut her off brutally, "the tour's just half over, and you still aren't willing to cooperate!"

"I was—"

"I don't care! You stay with me, or you can damn well make the rest of the trip without me!"

"Gib," she pleaded reasonably.

But he was beyond reason. And the worst part of it was that he could see himself out of control and was powerless to stop his behavior. She'd driven him beyond the bounds of patience. A still-functioning part of his brain was telling him that it wasn't her fault she was beautiful and innocent and that he lusted after her with painful desperation.

But he was no longer rational. "God, we have one free day and not only can we not relax, I have to chase you through the woods! You trying to convert the bears to virginity now?"

The confusion in her eyes fled as her own formidable temper ignited with blue flame. "You are hereby relieved of your duties, Mr. London," she said coldly. "This tour is now without a bodyguard." She raised her arms suddenly, trying to fling off his hands, but he held firm. Then he gave her a shake for good measure.

"You didn't hire me," he said, his anger now quiet. "I am on this tour for the duration, and you're going to cooperate. You're a virgin, but you're a woman, for God's sake. Stop running off on impulse like a child!"

He saw both her hands draw back, and he braced himself, certain he was about to get both of them across the face. But she changed her mind midswing, and both hands landed on his pectoral muscles with a vicious shove. He had to focus to hold his ground.

She was so angry he wouldn't have been surprised

if she'd caught fire. Her wild hair after their tussle even made it look a little as though she had.

And something about that served to quiet his temper. He didn't understand what it was, just that something in him seemed irrevocably tied to her, and even a negative reaction on her part made him aware of just how united they were.

He wasn't sure he liked that, in view of what he knew of man-woman relationships, but it was a reality he couldn't change.

"Don't you dare suggest," she warned in a low, quavering voice, "that my sexual inexperience in any way makes me more child than woman."

"That's not what I said," he disputed.

"Having sex is not a sign of maturity." She was on tiptoe now, her anger so complete she seemed to have to stretch herself to contain it. "In fact, having indiscriminate sex is a sign of *im*maturity. Of which you're a prime example."

"And you're qualified to judge the causes of indiscriminate sex when you haven't experienced it even once?"

"You don't have to be held underwater to know that you can drown."

He opened his mouth to answer, but was silenced by a small, high-pitched, repetitive whine drifting out of the woods behind them.

Kathy turned her head in its direction, then glowered at Gib. "*That's* what I came to investigate," she said. "I had no intention of messing with hibernation rituals." Then she ran off after the sound.

Resigned to his fate, Gib followed.

Kathy tracked the sound to a disintegrating cardboard box in the shelter of a maple tree. Inside were five yellow puppies, still too small to escape the box. She knelt beside it, reeling out a profane judgment of the dogs' owner that forced a smile from Gib.

"Who would do such a thing?" she demanded, picking up one puppy and holding it close to her face, uncaring of the dirt and leaves clinging to its fur. "You poor baby!" She picked up a second one and tried to hold two in one hand while reaching for a third.

It would have been more expedient to leave them in the box and carry the box back to the limo, but Gib knew she was thinking they were probably desperate for touch. And considering the way they nuzzled and rooted at her throat, she was probably right.

Gib picked up the other two and held them close, his mind already running ahead to what on earth they were going to do with them. How did one smuggle five whining puppies into a five-star hotel?

Kathy didn't care that they had no answer to that question. She looked at him with blood in her eye. "I'm taking them back to the limo," she said in the same tone David Farragut must have used when he damned the torpedoes.

Gib did have difficulty believing people could love, but his father had had a golden retriever who had loved Gib unconditionally and whom Gib had loved in return.

"Fine," he said.

She was losing the struggle to hold two puppies in one hand, and she looked at him suspiciously over them as she wrapped her arms around all of them. "And then what are we going to do with them?"

"I haven't a clue," he replied coolly. "I thought

a sexually inactive and mature person like yourself would have a solution."

She gave him an indignant glance. "Don't be snide."

His long hand confining two puppies to his chest, he reached to take her third puppy and place it in the large pocket of his coat. "Come on," he said, getting to his feet. "Maybe Sam can keep them for you until we figure out what to do."

She smiled hopefully. "You think?"

"Not usually. I'm generally considered an immature, indiscri—"

"Oh, shut up."

Sam, bless him, was an animal lover. "My kids will love to take care of them for you until the tour's over," he said, rubbing one small puppy body against his craggy cheek. "We have a big old farmhouse. Nothing fancy but lots of room, and we'll put a pile of blankets near the woodstove where they'll be nice and warm."

Kathy threw her arms around him. "Thank you, *thank* you, Sam!"

He patted her back with a giant hand. "Happy to help, Miss McQuade."

"OH, GOOD," Patsy said with a thin smile when Kathy recounted the morning's adventures, prudently leaving out her argument with Gib. He was downstairs with the concierge, checking out restaurants for dinner. "Five golden Labrador puppies is just what our crowded apartment needs."

Kathy made a face at her. "They might be golden retrievers. I'm not sure."

Patsy sighed. "Even better. Longer hair." Then

she wrapped her arms around Kathy and leaned back to smile at her. "Actually, I'm delighted to see you loosening up. This tour is having a good effect on you. Tell me, Bacall, is it Bogey?"

"Oh, right," she said, going to the small kitchen to make tea. "I'd like to make a hole in his *African Queen* and watch him sink!"

"That was Bogart and Hepburn."

"Well, punch out his *Maltese Falcon,* then."

"That was Bogart and Mary Astor."

Kathy turned to her mother impatiently. "The comparison isn't going to work, anyway. If there's anything I'm not, it's sultry."

Patsy wrinkled her brow. "I thought you were starting to get along."

"Yeah, me, too." Kathy filled the kettle, turned on the burner and pulled two cups out of the overhead cupboard. "But you should have heard him lay into me this morning when I heard the puppies and went into the woods. One minute we were walking along arm in arm, and the next minute he was screaming at me."

Patsy had curled up in a corner of the sofa and Kathy sank onto the cushion beside her.

"I'm not surprised." Patsy leaned her elbow on the back of the sofa and returned Kathy's startled look. "What? Did you think he'd stay an arm's length away from you every day for weeks and not be affected by that? You're a very beautiful young woman, and when you're not being a twit, you have charm and wit and all kinds of other things that appeal to a man like Gib."

Kathy shook her head, then leaned it against the back of the sofa. "I thought so for a while. I even hoped so. But now I think I just annoy him. And why not? I mean, he annoys me and I'm pretty hard to annoy. He suggested today that I'm immature."

Patsy patted her head. "It's part of your charm."

"Mother..."

"Sorry. Go on."

"Maybe one thing not having sex does for you is that it helps you retain the girlish image of the perfect man, and maybe that's not a good thing." She heaved a discontented sigh. "I've wanted to be married for a long time. I think I'm the kind of woman who'd be happiest with a husband and children. But I kept thinking this wonderful, perfect being would come along who'd be in complete harmony with me and I'd recognize him instantly."

Patsy leaned a little closer to her. "Honey, true harmony comes from different sounds, not from the same sound. If you marry someone just like you, your life would be dull indeed. There would be no surprises.

"Incidentally, Neil called four times. The last time he deigned to speak to me and said to tell you he's going to get a little free time and meet us in Phoenix."

Kathy frowned thoughtfully. "Maybe it's time I took his advances more seriously."

Patsy put a hand to her head and groaned theatrically. "Why don't you just feed me antifreeze or tie explosives to my chest or—"

"Mother! Get a grip."

Gib chose that moment to return, and Kathy felt all her defenses go up, preparing to hold her decision in place. It was a sound decision, so she couldn't imagine why she felt as though she'd been placed in the middle of the Alaskan wilderness without a dog-sled. Or a dog.

"Gib, come quickly!" her mother said, sitting up. "She's talking about marrying Neil! Talk some sense into her, will you?"

He wore gray slacks and a soft, dark blue sweater, which added its color to the green and brown in his eyes. He fell gracefully into a chair opposite the sofa and said with smiling calm, "I'm sure she'll come to her senses before she actually does it. He's just using her for her book."

"Aha!" Patsy jabbed the air with her index finger. "That's what I'm always telling her, but she won't listen to me."

"She won't listen to anybody," Gib said without passion. "I have daily proof of that. But one day she'll realize that his only interest in her is that she appeals to his conservative New England constituency and can help him get elected."

"That *isn't* true!" Kathy insisted. "There are any number of attractive single women who could do more for him politically than I can."

"But virginity's a timely subject," Gib said. "Wait and see. When the tour's over, he'll proposition you, not propose to you. He looks at you with lust, Kathy, not love."

"Your interest in me," Kathy said with strained forbearance, "is how much money I can make for London Publishing. How does that differ from Neil's interest in me, if you are right about him?"

He looked into her eyes, and for a moment she thought he was on the brink of confessing something, admitting something. Then he replied, mercilessly, she thought. "I'm not claiming to love you."

Anger rose in her like fireworks. "And that's a good thing, too, isn't it, since you wouldn't know love if you fell over it!"

"Maybe. I've never had it."

"No, you don't want to be bothered with it, and that's a different thing entirely." Kathy got to her feet, energy suddenly spent. "I'm going to take a nap before dinner."

"Call me," he teased gently, "if there's anyone in your closet."

Chapter Nine

Kathy, Gib and Patsy were up at 6:00 a.m. for Kathy's nine o'clock appearance on a morning magazine show.

Kathy awoke in the doldrums from yesterday's argument with Gib, but by the time she'd had makeup applied, her hairstyle refined, been fed a bagel and a mocha, she was feeling more positive.

Many difficult things had happened on the tour, and she'd handled all of them at least competently. She was holding her own just fine.

And she could continue to do so with or without Gib London. She felt as though ground gave way inside of her at that thought. It wasn't just that they disagreed so completely about life and love that upset her. It was that she now felt as though he was everything she needed, everything she'd been looking for—despite his attitude—yet he could look her in the eye and say with complete conviction, "I'm not claiming to love you."

Which was a good thing, she told herself. Honesty was important, even when it hurt.

But she couldn't help thinking it would have felt

wonderful to be able to believe that he cared just a little.

Her mother insisted that the volatile argument yesterday had occurred because he *was* affected by their closeness, but if that was simply sexual, who cared? And who could put faith in her mother's grasp of romance, anyway? She'd trusted Jack Trent after all.

As Kathy waited to go before the camera, she made a resolution. If this tour was successful, her life would be moving forward professionally, if not personally. And she would dedicate herself to that. She would get her mother out of debt, continue to work in the bookstore while she spent her free time writing fiction, and hopefully one day it would all pay off.

She and her mother would live together in a house filled with yellow dogs on a hill overlooking the bay, and she would be very happy. Her mother was a terrible buttinsky but they got along well. Life would be good. She would be happy. Very happy.

Buoyed by the image, she walked confidently onstage as her name was announced.

The host and hostess, Max and Marcie Blaine, were a young married couple well-known for their witty byplay and unusual guests. Kathy braced herself, half expecting to be interviewed as an oddity rather than as a woman with hopeful, logical views.

She was pleasantly surprised when the interview began with the reading of her book and positive reviews of Kathy's appearances collected over the two weeks she'd been touring.

Cordelia had gotten in touch with her several times since she'd been on the road to assure her that responses so far were favorable and that sales were exceeding even their greatest expectations.

But most of the publicity had resulted from Gib's presence on the tour.

She was relieved, therefore, when Max began asking about her parents rather than her bodyguard. She would have had difficulty discussing him with neutrality.

"Your father was a printer, I understand," he said.

"That's right."

Marcie winked at the audience. "There's a charming story about how her parents met. Why don't you tell our audience, Kathy?"

Relaxing, Kathy launched into the long-familiar tale of how her mother, working part-time for Bayside Pizza while she was in college, delivered a pizza to the print shop where her father was employed and where she eventually went to work.

"Unfortunately," she told the audience with a laugh, "the delivery time happened to coincide with the moment an outraged client, upset over personal problems as well as a four-fold job that had been printed partially upside down, walked into the shop with a gun."

Marcie gasped. Max hung on Kathy's every word. The studio audience waited in anticipation.

"My father," Kathy went on, "in a back room, heard what was happening and hid under the desk with the telephone and called the police. When my mother walked in through the back with the pizza, he pulled her under the desk with him until the police arrived."

The audience and Max and Marcie laughed. "It

was lust and pizza in the knee hole of a desk?'' Max asked.

''Something like that,'' Kathy replied. ''My father always said that he'd ordered a pizza with everything on it that day, and it came with a wife.''

''And gunshots!'' Marcie exclaimed, eyes wide with pretended fright as the audience laughed even more.

Kathy shook her head. ''No shots were fired. The gun wasn't even loaded, mercifully.''

Max smiled with her over that, then consulted a small stack of notes on the coffee table in front of Kathy's chair. ''So, you were raised with traditional family values, according to your bio.''

''That's right.''

''And that's where the material from your book came from.''

''No, not precisely. I was working on my thesis for a masters in sociology and was researching the effect of promiscu—''

Max frowned suddenly. ''Because I was wondering,'' he interrupted, an index finger raised then tapped against his mouth as he appeared to be thinking. Then he went on, assuming an air of apology, ''how we can equate that claim with the fact that you were born only four months after your parents' wedding day?''

Kathy was aware of the smile frozen on her face. She'd been the victim several times on this tour of friendly questions that really harbored a trap to make her look silly, or phony, or something else likely to liven up a show.

But she'd never experienced direct lies before.

She reminded herself that she was speaking not

just to Max and Marcie, but several hundred-thousand people and forced a calm, polite tone of voice.

"You're mistaken, Max. I was born in April, and my parents were married the previous June."

He and Marcie looked at each other with what appeared to be sympathy. "Your parents were married in December, Kathy," Marcie said gravely. "On the twelfth. Is it possible that you didn't know?"

Kathy opened her mouth to insist again that they were wrong when Max pulled a formal-looking document from the middle of his notes. He handed it to Kathy.

Anger was so explosive inside her that she had to concentrate to focus on the document, to remember that letters made words and words would eventually make sense.

It was a copy of a marriage certificate with all the blanks filled in.

It said: "Robert Matthew McQuade married Patricia Elaine Barlow on this—" Kathy stared at the date, then read it again "—on this twelfth day of December in the year of Our Lord nineteen hundred and seventy-two."

December. Kathy continued to stare at it.

Confusion ran over her anger and seemed to want to settle in every corner of her being so that she couldn't figure out what it was, or what it meant.

Then she looked up instinctively toward the edge of the set, where Gib and her mother watched, and saw her mother's hands over her mouth, then her impulsive step toward Kathy.

Gib stopped her and pulled her back.

And suddenly Kathy understood what Max was doing.

She marshaled all the forces of strength and control that she'd gathered over the years in a life that really hadn't required all that many and prayed they would be enough.

She turned to Max with a small smile as she handed back the wedding certificate. "It seems I was the one who was mistaken."

"So you didn't know you were an *early* baby?" Marcie emphasized the word *early* with a look and a tone so exploitatively empathetic that it took all Kathy's self-control not to slap her.

"No, I didn't," she replied. "I was too busy being a happy baby, a well-loved baby. There were never two kinder, finer people in the world than my parents."

"But your mother was preg—"

Kathy nodded and cut her off. "Marcie, my mother didn't write *The Virgin Returns*. I did. And my book in no way devalues women who've made other choices for whatever reasons. It just suggests that virginity would eliminate a lot of problems with which our lives are overrun—unwanted children, dangerous diseases, relationships that never have a chance to develop because of the pressures sex puts upon them before a couple even knows what each other is all about."

She paused because she needed desperately to breathe. She looked from one host to the other. "Virginity, however, can't do anything about people willing to shock or embarrass other people before the public for purposes of personal gain. That's unfortunate."

The audience roared on Kathy's behalf. Max stammered for a moment, then went quickly to commercial.

Kathy unhooked her microphone and placed it on her chair.

"Kathy, you have to understand," Max said, blocking her way as she tried to leave the set. "It's nothing personal, but if you're not who you claim to be, it's our duty to inform the—"

Max got no further. A fist shot out from over Kathy's shoulder and knocked him to the floor.

Marcie shrieked and knelt over her husband as Gib, rubbing his knuckles, bent over Max. "The next time your duty involves embarrassing two women on the air," he warned, "you'd better make damn sure I'm not waiting off camera."

Gib took Kathy's arm and marched her off the set, reaching for Patsy, too, as they headed for the door. He ushered them into the limo, then climbed in behind them.

There was silence as Sam closed their door, walked around the limo to the driver's side and looked over his shoulder at Gib. "I was watching the TV in the back," he said with a sympathetic frown. "Back to the hotel?"

Gib gave him a grim smile. "You think we can beat the reporters there?"

Sam nodded and turned the key in the ignition with purpose. "Watch me," he called over his shoulder. "But if I'm wrong, I'll get you in the service entrance and up the freight elevator. Don't worry about a thing."

Don't worry about a thing. Kathy decided she

could relate to that philosophy. There was now far too much to worry about to concentrate on *one* thing.

Her mother was crying.

Kathy looped an arm in hers. "It's going to be all right, Mom," she lied.

"Oh, how can it possibly all right?" Patsy wept, taking the handkerchief Gib handed her, too distracted to say thank you. "Now I've made you into one of the very statistics your book is trying to warn young women against."

Kathy patted her arm. "You didn't write the book, Mom. I did. You're not responsible for anything."

"Of course I'm responsible. You know how the media is. It'll *affect* everything. First they'll speculate on whether or not you knew, then they'll say you had to have known and suggest that you were trying to put something over on your reading public by keeping it from them. Then someone will insinuate that Bogey and Bacall are shacked up and taking the public for a ride. Then Max will sue Gib and London Publishing and each of the aunts separately, and..."

Gib had reached into the small liquor compartment beside him and poured half a glass of champagne, which he handed to Patsy. "Drink this," he ordered calmly, "and try not to be such an optimist."

He poured another glass and handed it to Kathy. She tried to refuse it, but he put it into her free hand. "Drink it," he said. "You're the color of recycled paper."

Kathy didn't want to take it because she was afraid her hand would shake, and she didn't want anyone to know how deeply she'd been affected by what had just happened. It wasn't the embarrassment of being ambushed by the news on television, it was the fact that her life had begun differently than she'd thought, and the people she'd loved and trusted since the day she was born hadn't told her the truth.

Everything was askew, teetering on the edge, maybe even lying on its side with its gas tank leaking.

"Drink it," Gib said sharply.

Kathy complied, relieved that she could get the bowl of the glass to her lips without spilling it.

Her mother downed her glass in two gulps, and Gib refilled it.

"It wasn't that we...I...we ever intended to lie to you," Patsy said. "Thank you, Gib. It was that we were such a happy little unit there seemed little point in it by the time you were old enough to understand. We were a solid family."

Kathy took another sip. It warmed a little line down to her stomach, but it wasn't enough to dispel the cold that seemed to be seeping in everywhere.

"You told me your anniversary was June 12," Kathy reminded her.

Patsy shrugged. "There were no relatives around to disprove it, and you were such an inquisitive little thing, I was sure you'd know what it meant if I'd told you the truth."

"I thought you weren't ashamed of it."

Her glass empty again, Patsy held it out to Gib for a refill. He obliged.

"I was born in the forties, darling, of course I was ashamed of it. Not of loving your...your father, of course, but of ignoring the rules. I just didn't see any reason why I should tell you when it seemed impossible that the issue would ever come up. Ha!'' She expelled a deep sigh and frowned forlornly. ''How could I know that one day you would write a book on virginity, and that my secret would bite us both in the derriere on live television?'' Patsy turned to Kathy, her eyes glazed with misery. ''You hate me, don't you?''

''Of course not.''

''You will when the shock wears off.''

''I'm fine. We'll all be fine.''

Sam called the hotel and learned that there were reporters in the lobby. He drove around the back where the freight elevator was ready to whisk them up to their floor.

''We owe you big, Sam,'' Gib said as he saw Kathy and Patsy into their suite.

Sam shook his head. ''Maybe just a puppy. What time we leaving for the airport in the morning?''

''Seven.''

''I'll be here. Wait for me to come up. If there are reporters, we'll go down the same way.''

''Good plan.''

GIB HATED not knowing what to do. Generally he understood women very well. They were warm, charming, interesting, and most of the ones in his life expected little from him but opera tickets and good sex.

But in the short time he'd spent with Kathy and Patsy, he'd come to know them better than he'd known any woman who'd crossed his path, except perhaps his mother, his aunts and Mrs. Conway.

And his mother had never really known *him.*

Patsy was witty, trusting, enthusiastic and loved her daughter with every breath she drew.

Kathy was idealistic, skeptical, curious and loved her mother just as deeply.

He now considered Patsy his friend and was afraid to analyze too closely how he felt about Kathy. But he knew he hated to see them at odds. Though Kathy was trying hard to be understanding of what had happened, she had to be affected by it and probably needed the opportunity to get it off her chest.

Instead, she'd changed into her jade sweatsuit and made a pot of coffee. He knew when she ignored the packet of Irish cream for the more robust fog-lifter blend that she was desperate.

Patsy, riddled with guilt, tried to help.

"I'll do it, Mom," Kathy said. "Why don't you take a bath or a nap?"

"Because I need to talk," Patsy said, catching Kathy's hands. "Don't you want to talk?"

"About what?" Kathy asked amiably. "It would have been nice if you'd told me, but you didn't. And it doesn't really change anything, anyway."

"Just...tell me what you're thinking."

"I'm thinking that it doesn't matter!"

Gib thought such a forcefully spoken denial said just the opposite, and Patsy's maternal instinct saw it, too.

"I think it does," Patsy insisted, "and you don't want to hurt me. But we're going to have to discuss it if we're going to go on together. Aren't you even a little afraid of what it's going to do to the rest of the tour? Maybe I should give an interview and explain that..."

The ring of the telephone interrupted her suggestion. Gib went toward it, but Kathy, apparently eager to escape her mother's well-meaning talk, hurried to reach it first.

"Hello." She leaned a hip on the edge of the sofa, then straightened and beckoned to Patsy. "Yes, she is. Just a moment."

She handed her mother the phone, then went back into the kitchen.

Patsy sat on the arm of the sofa and answered with mild impatience. "Yes?" Then she got slowly to her feet, an expression of disbelief in her eyes as they looked up at Kathy. "Jack? I can't believe it! How did you find us?"

Kathy came around the counter to stand in the kitchen doorway, frowning. She looked suddenly tense, her cheeks pink, her fists closed tightly as though she was on the brink of some kind of explosion.

"Well..." Patsy turned her back to Kathy, her voice high, her words quick. "But how can you? Where are you? We're in Denver and you're..." She sat down again and finished weakly, "You're in Denver? But I don't understand." She listened for a few moments, darted a guilty look at Kathy, then glanced at the clock above the kitchen counter. "Yes. Yes, I'll be here. But we've had a little trouble with... Oh, you did?" A little shrug in Kathy's direction. "Yes, I know. No, we're fine." She got up and walked to the window that looked down on a busy street. "I'll meet you across the street at a little Italian place called Denio's. Yes. All right. Two o'clock. 'Bye, Jack." Patsy cradled the receiver, then turned to smile thinly at Kathy. "That was Jack."

"No kidding." Kathy remained where she stood, the frown firmly in place. "And you're meeting him at two, even though he lied to you and stole from you."

"Kathy." Patsy stood, a sudden resolve firming her features. "There's more to him than you understand. I told you he'd come back. And when I wasn't in Bayside, he set out to find me."

Kathy made a scornful sound. "Of course he did. You're on a book tour with the potential of making money. Now he can steal even more from you."

"I told you I'm not taking any of this money. And that's not why he's here."

They now looked to Gib like two goddesses at war, the younger one determined to wrestle control. He half expected to see lightning bolts fly from Kathy's index finger as she pointed it at Patsy.

"You're falling for it again."

"I'm not falling for anything, I'm trusting."

Kathy raised both arms in complete frustration. "Trusting? Really? Well, I did that and let me tell you something about it. You should keep your powder dry."

Kathy started off toward her room.

"Kathryn Victoria McQuade, you stop right there!" Patsy shouted.

Kathy stopped and spun around, red hair flying out, her expression thunderous.

"I understand how you feel about what happened today," Patsy said, her voice a little unsteady, "but it's no reason to stop trusting me. I didn't tell you when you got older because I didn't think you'd understand. You just decided on the high road and took it because...because...'' Patsy hesitated, clearly having difficulty finding the right words.

''Because celibacy is easy for me?'' Kathy demanded. ''Because I have no passion? Is that what you're trying to say?''

Before Patsy could answer, Kathy had stormed out of the suite.

Gib didn't even wait for Patsy's helpless, pleading look in his direction before following her daughter into the hallway.

He caught Kathy by the back of her sweatshirt on her way to the elevators and dodged her fist as it flew out at him. ''I'm going *out!*'' she shouted at him.

''Fine,'' he said, anchoring her to his side and lifting her feet clear of the carpet. He turned in the direction of the freight elevator. ''But unless you want to explain to a group of scandal-hungry reporters why you're sobbing and running away, we'd better go out the back.''

''I don't...need a bodyguard to take a walk!'' She squirmed and struggled against him, but he dragged her relentlessly with him.

A waiter was coming off the elevator with a room-service cart and held the door for them while Gib lifted Kathy into the car. The waiter gave one quick glance to her, then smiled at Gib as the doors began to close.

''Mine's like that, too,'' he said. ''Got to pin her down to get her attention.''

''Yours?'' Kathy shouted futilely at the waiter as the doors closed. ''Like she's a pet or a thing? What if I was being kidnapped? What if...?''

"He's gone, Kathy," Gib said quietly from a corner of the car. It was moving downward.

Her shoulders sagged and she put a hand to her forehead, the picture of dejection.

Sympathy for her filled him.

No. It was more than that. Sympathy wouldn't grind his feelings, allow him to feel her pain, make him think he would give anything—maybe even his careful neutrality—if it would kill that lost look in her eyes.

Well. There it was. The truth he'd been dodging for days. He'd lived with his neutrality since he'd awakened from a nightmare at four years old and no one had come in response to his screams. He never considered giving it up for anybody.

He was in love with Kathy McQuade.

A string of bad words came to mind, but he was in the presence of a virgin. Although he guessed she might even be considering a few herself.

He caught her hand and pulled her into his shoulder. "Try to calm down," he suggested softly, rubbing her rigid upper arm. "I know it's been a lousy day, but you were the epitome of class and style through it all. Try to remember that your mother would die before she'd willingly hurt you. And so would I." She looked at him in cautious surprise, and he added with a grin. "Well, I love to harass you, but I won't let anybody else hurt you."

She looked surprised, but that was gone in an instant and she smiled flatly. "That's a comfort." But she didn't pull away.

The doors parted on the bottom floor, Gib and Kathy stepped out of the car and were halfway to the service exit when someone behind them shouted, "There they go!"

Gib looked over his shoulder, spotting reporters and photographers pouring from the lobby down the long corridor toward him and Kathy. He pushed Kathy through the open exit door, then caught her hand and ran.

She kept up with him for a block, then pleaded in a high voice, "Gib, you've been dragging me the last hundred feet!"

He rounded the corner and ducked into the first storefront. It was a deli, the atmosphere redolent of spiced meats, honey-cured ham and freshly baked bread.

They hid behind a tall rack of assorted chips and watched as the small crowd of reporters and photographers stopped in front of the store, peered through the window, milled around for a few minutes while looking up and down the street, clearly having lost their quarry. Then someone shouted, pointing back in the direction from which they'd come, "There! Red hair!" And they were off en masse.

Kathy was leaning against Gib and breathing heavily. "Are they gone?" she asked as he looked cautiously over the chips rack for any indication of stragglers. There were none.

"Yes," he said, feeling like James Bond again. Only this time, not quite so much like a cheap imitation. "All gone."

She looked up at him with an expression of relief, and he was pleased to see that the sudden excitement had diluted the day's upsets.

She took a whiff of the aromatic air and put a hand to her stomach.

"Hungry?" he asked.

"Yeah." Kathy looked up at a menu board posted on the wall behind the counter. Her brain was still scrambled, however, and seemed unwilling to make a decision about anything.

Gib drew her toward a corner table covered in strawberry-patterned oilcloth. "Sit down," he said, pulling a chair out for her. "Don't think about anything. I'll be right back."

Don't think about anything. She repeated his words to herself as he went to the broad counter where a tall, bulky man, wrapped in a huge white apron, waited with smiling patience.

How could she not think about anything? All she could *do* was think. Ever since Max Blaine had told her her parents were married only four months before she was born, she'd been trying to make sense of the contents of her store of knowledge.

Her brain seemed to be going round and round—proof, she thought, that at this point in time it was operated by a gerbil and not a Pentium chip.

Not that being an "early" baby was such an outrageous or even an original circumstance, but she found herself wondering if her sudden presence in the world had forced two people into a situation they wouldn't have chosen.

But her parents had been happy. They'd *seemed* happy. Of course, her last memory of her father was collected when she was nine years old, so what did she really know?

Maybe it had all been a performance for her benefit. Otherwise—why wouldn't someone have told her?

The gerbil in her head ran furiously on his going-nowhere path until Gib returned to the table with two giant sandwiches on paper plates. They'd been secured with a toothpick adorned with a green olive, a pearl onion and a tiny radish. A pile of crunchy chips filled up the remaining space on the plate.

As Gib placed her plate before her, she lifted one edge of a triangle of fragrant, sourdough bread, and her brain finally began to calculate: two one-ounce slices each of ham, pastrami, roast beef, and a thick slice of provolone slathered with herbed mayo and Dijon on two slices of sourdough at least eight inches across, teamed with a good four ounces of thickly sliced kettle chips, salt-and-vinegar flavored, and she was looking at two thousand calories. At least.

That was when she discovered that though her brain was working, her conscience was unplugged. She made a sound of pleasure, picked up the giant doorstop of a sandwich and opened her mouth.

Gib reached out quickly, snatched off the toothpick that was about to make it possible for her to wear a nose ring, and dropped it on her plate. He grinned at her as he picked up his own sandwich. "Good," he said. "I was afraid you were going to moan and complain about the calories. But there's nothing like fat and carbo loading when you're upset."

Kathy nodded as she chewed, then swallowed. "I hope they have cheesecake. Delis usually have cheesecake."

"Several flavors. You can try them all. Eat up."

Gib's plate was clean and Kathy was several bites into the second half of her sandwich before her desperate need for nourishment began to abate. She wasn't sure whether to be pleased about it or not because brain function was definitely returning.

She pushed the sandwich away, picked up the toothpick and pulled the olive off with her teeth. She chewed it slowly, enjoying the slightly oily, savory taste.

"I wonder," she said idly, studying the onion and the radish still adorning the toothpick, "if my parents would have married if my mother hadn't become pregnant with me."

"Come on," he chided gently. "Every word your mother ever says about your father relates to how much she loved him. How much they loved each other. How happy they were. You must remember that."

She nipped the onion off with her teeth and ate it. It made her eyes water and caught at the back of her throat. She coughed.

Gib pushed her can of cola toward her. "You're not going to hold that against them?"

She gave him an impatient glance. "Of course not. I just think it would have been nice if someone had told me. It's my life. I mean, to lie to me for twenty-six years about the date of their wedding anniversary."

"Maybe their love started on that day," he suggested. "Maybe that's what they were celebrating, and it wasn't really a lie after all. A wedding's something you do for each other. A priest or a minister officiates, but technically you don't need them. You say the vows. You make the promises."

She sighed, thinking that all sounded very logical, but she couldn't dismiss this new feeling of being a mistake. "Even so, nobody plans to have a child out of wedlock. It usually happens because birth control fails, or it's a simple error in judgment."

Gib leaned toward her over the rubble of their lunches. "I'm sure there are lots of people walking around who were conceived *after* marriages had taken place, but also without having been planned."

"And they probably all feel like I do—as though they might have messed up a relationship rather than having been a gift to it."

"That's nonsense and you know it." His quiet tone of voice blunted the merciless quality of the words. "You know they loved each other and they both adored you. There's nothing here that diminishes you in any way, so stop looking for it. And stop being angry at your mother."

She met his direct gaze with an angry flare in her own. "I'm not looking for martyr material. And you've been mad at your parents your whole life, why can't I be mad at mine?"

He raised an eyebrow. "I'm neutral about my parents."

She nodded. "A child's most punishing payback. Don't get holier-than-thou with me when you've been on a lifelong pout."

He studied her darkly for one moment, then he leaned back in his chair. "And for that bad behavior, missy," he said, "you get no cheesecake."

She made a scornful sound, got to her feet and went to the counter to order two pieces on her own and two cups of coffee. She brought them back to the table and placed one in front of him, then held her right hand out toward him, palm up. "I didn't bring any money," she said defensively, "but I'll pay you back."

He put a ten into her palm.

The desserts paid for, Kathy returned to her chair. She stabbed the cheesecake with her fork, took a bite, savored it with a groan of approval, then swallowed it and put her fork down to renew their argument.

"My mother said she didn't tell me because she didn't think I'd understand. That hurts."

Gib, half his cheesecake already gone, sipped at his coffee. "I suppose she thought that...since you've never been in love you wouldn't understand the strong feelings involved."

"Of course I do. You don't have to be kissed by Mel Gibson to know it would be wonderful."

He frowned, distracted. "I never thought so."

"Think about kissing Julia Roberts."

He seemed to be thinking, then made a sound of uncertainty.

"Jennifer Anniston?"

He made that sound again.

"What?" she asked tolerantly. "Wrong hair color? Wrong height?"

He shrugged easily. "Wrong woman," he replied, then took another sip of coffee.

"Well, I was just trying to make a po—" There was something in his eyes she'd never seen there before.

Deliberate seduction.

The night they'd danced in New Orleans, the camera had caught his expression by surprise. But this afternoon he knew it was there.

An electric charge went up and down her spine and temporarily shorted out her newly reloaded brain.

What did this mean? What? That she'd been right all along? That he felt something for her?

Never one to hedge a bet, she swallowed and asked boldly, "You think kissing...*me* would be wonderful."

He added a grin to that soft-eyed roving look, and its effect was devastating to her entire physical and emotional makeup. "I know it is," he replied. "I've done it. Or have you forgotten?"

She stared at him in disbelief for a full ten seconds. "No," she whispered finally, "I haven't."

"Good." He finished off his coffee. "Just making sure." He crushed the foam cup in his hand and put it on the tray, collecting the rest of their leftovers, as well. Then he leaned over it to say seriously, himself once again, "About your mom. I think sometimes strong people don't understand other people's weaknesses where love is concerned, and she might have thought you'd be somehow disappointed in her."

She stared at him for just an instant, wondering if she'd imagined that delicious grin. But her brain *was* working again, and she knew she hadn't. For reasons best known to him, he didn't want to deal with it now.

Which was fine with her. Two personal crises were more than she could deal with in one day. So she eased back into their old footing and challenged him.

"Really," she said doubtfully, tossing her now-empty cup and her napkin onto the tray. "And how would *you* come to that conclusion? You'd have to understand feelings of being in love, and you don't believe in it."

She caught a glimpse of that soft-eyed look again, but this time it was tinged with an expression that suggested impending doom. "Maybe I'm beginning to," he replied, and carried their tray to the counter.

Chapter Ten

It took two hours to walk off the sandwich and the cheesecake, but when Gib hailed a cab to take them back to the hotel, Kathy still wasn't ready.

"I don't want anything to do with Jack Trent," she said stubbornly, resisting Gib's tug on her arm as a bright yellow cab with a mountain scene painted on the side pulled up to the curb.

"Your mother's an intelligent woman, Kathy." Gib leaned down to pull the back door open. "I think you can trust her to manage her own life."

Kathy turned her back to the cab and frowned up at Gib. "He stole her car, her money and her heart!"

Gib nodded grimly. "So you've told me. But if *she* wants to see him again, it's possible he gave her something you don't know about or understand."

Kathy spread her arms helplessly. "Oh, of course. The virgin doesn't understand *anything*."

He smiled—a gentle, affectionate, accepting smile. "No, it's that the virgin doesn't always have the answer to everything. And it doesn't matter how well ordered you try to make your life, or how perfectly you set it up to ward off mishaps or disasters, they're going to happen. And everyone has to deal with them in the way they feel is appropriate."

"Hey!" the cabbie called, leaning backward over the front seat to look out at them through the open back door. "You're up to $6.50 and we haven't even left the curb yet!"

With an exasperated sigh, Kathy climbed into the cab.

Gib followed, gave the cabbie the address of the hotel as he closed and locked their door, and they were off through the waning light of late afternoon.

John Denver's "Rocky Mountain High" filled the cab with loud but mellow music.

"I think she's wrong," Kathy insisted. "And I will not stand by and let him hurt her again."

Gib patted her hand between them on the seat. "I'm sure that alone will prevent him from doing it. I can't imagine he came back with bad intentions, when he knows she could put him in jail in a minute."

Kathy frowned over that.

Then her mother's problems fled her mind as her memory flashed a picture of the look Gib had given her in the deli. She felt that same electrical charge all over again.

There was a sudden change of atmosphere in the back of the cab, a thinness to the air, an enveloping quality to the music that seemed to wrap itself around them, make a knot and tighten it.

She turned to Gib to see if he was aware of the same things.

He had leaned his head against the back of the seat and closed his eyes. "Don't even mention it," he said without opening them.

She frowned at his handsome, quiet face. "That's a mature way to deal with it."

He smiled, still without opening his eyes. "The mature way to deal with it would negate all the work you've done on this tour and make mincemeat of all the good advice in your book."

She laughed lightly. "You mean I'd be helpless to withstand your seduction?"

He did open his eyes at that, and she was surprised to find a serious expression in them. "No," he replied. "I'd be helpless to withstand you, and that would be worse. Just leave it alone for now."

She opened her mouth to protest, but he'd already closed his eyes again.

She leaned close to him, frustrated and annoyed. "I'm going to tell your aunts how much of your job you did with your eyes closed."

He smiled again. "It's my only defense against you."

And that was a lie, he thought as he felt the cab slow down as the downtown traffic thickened. Because he could still see her, even with his eyes closed. It was as though she'd seeped into his pores, altered the components of his body so that his whole awareness was filled with her.

Oh, God.

JACK TRENT DIDN'T LOOK like a bad sort, Gib thought as he and Kathy entered the hotel suite. Patsy and her companion, seated facing each other on the sofa, turned in their direction and got to their feet. In fact, Gib thought he saw something somehow familiar in the man's eyes, something he'd once known or felt.

Gib rubbed Kathy lightly between the shoulder-blades to push her inside, then closed the door behind them.

"Did you avoid the reporters?" Patsy asked.

When Kathy didn't answer, Gib did. "We lost them on the way out and there was no one in the lobby when we came in."

Patsy smiled thinly. "That's because I promised them we'd give them an interview tomorrow. And this time, I'll do all the talking."

Kathy shook her head. "You don't have to explain yourself to anyone. I'll—"

"I know." Patsy raised both hands placatingly. "You'd like to handle damage control yourself, but I got you into this, and it's my responsibility to get you out." Her expression turned from placating to pleading. "It's really not an ugly story, just...not very original. Two kids too much in love to think twice. And you were always loved, Kathy, from the moment I suspected you. You were never considered something that shouldn't have happened."

Kathy dropped her purse and jacket onto a nearby chair and crossed the room to take Patsy into her arms. "I know. All I remember of my entire life has been love." She drew back to touch Patsy's face, then she pushed back, folded her arms and became suddenly severe. "That's why I don't want you to throw away that love on someone who should be behind bars."

Gib saw Jack Trent's mouth quirk in wry resignation. He understood that look. Kathy often made him feel it, too.

Trent was tall and lean, looking well muscled despite a thick thatch of gray hair. His eyes were dark and mournful, with occasional flickers of humor. Gib knew now where he'd seen that look. It had been in the eyes of the refugees in Somalia who no longer knew where they belonged.

"Hi, Kathy," Trent said in a deep, gravelly voice. "It's good to see you."

Kathy stared at him, unrelenting. "I'd like to say the same about you, Jack, but you stole from my mother. And you used love to do it. That's despicable."

Jack nodded. Patsy wrapped an arm around his waist and leaned into him. He leaned back, kissing the top of her head. "I'd like to talk to you about that."

"Well." Kathy dusted off her hands as though she was done with the situation. "I'd just as soon not have to listen." And she stalked off in the direction of her room.

Gib caught her arm and drew her back, reaching toward Trent, hand extended. There was something going on here, he thought, that Kathy wasn't seeing.

"Hi," he said. "Gib London. I'm touring with Kathy and her mom."

Trent looked surprised for a moment, then shook his hand. "Jack Trent. I guess Kathy's told you all about me."

He had a solid, callused handshake, Gib noticed. "Yeah," he admitted candidly. "You didn't come off very well. I think you deserve a chance to tell us your side."

"I appreciate that."

"We'll make a pot of coffee," Gib offered.

Patsy gave Gib a quick, grateful hug. "It's already

made. But you can get two more cups and top ours up.''

Kathy followed Gib into the tiny kitchen. ''You had no right to do that!'' she whispered harshly.

''It never hurts to talk something through,'' he said, pulling cups down. ''You might learn something you didn't know before.''

''Really.'' She grabbed the coffeepot and challenged him with a look. ''This from the man who told me in the cab not to 'even mention it.' Depends on how comfortable *you* are with the subject, doesn't it?''

He took the hit without flinching. ''That's different.''

''Of course it is.'' She walked away, nose in the air.

Kathy took one of the chairs opposite her mother, and Gib took the other. There was something in the atmosphere of the room that gave him a vague feeling of foreboding, but he put that up to the fact that he was in love. It wasn't natural. His systems—physical and emotional—didn't know what to do with the cheer that tried to pervade his being, the weird helplessness he experienced every time he looked at Kathy that should have made him feel weak but instead seemed to imbue him with a strange power.

He knew his instincts were right when Patsy leaned forward, elbows on her knees, and looked Kathy in the eye. ''Darling,'' she said, her voice beginning to tremble. ''We have something to tell you.''

Kathy had kicked off her shoes and tucked her feet up under her. Her upper body stiffened in the chair as though she, too, suspected it was going to be something momentous.

"Mom," she said in a flip tone, "how bad can it be? You can't be pregnant at your age, can you?"

Patsy's joined hands clenched until her knuckles were white and she replied a little weakly, "Funny you should say that."

Kathy was as still and unmoving as stone. Then she asked in a whisper, "What?"

Jack put a hand to Patsy's back and rubbed gently. Patsy seemed to take courage from that and drew a breath. "Of course I'm not pregnant, but...I did once carry Jack's baby."

Kathy stared, openmouthed, waiting for her to go on.

Patsy swallowed and said quickly, pleadingly, "That was you, Kathy."

The words had seemed to erupt into the air and vibrate there one long, protracted moment.

Kathy didn't react, but she held up her coffee cup as though looking for someplace to put it.

Gib went to take the hot coffee from her and placed it on the coffee table. Then he settled on the arm of her chair. She felt grateful for that.

"Robert McQuade was my father," she finally said, her tone stubborn and a little high.

Patsy nodded. "Yes, he was. And he was wonderful. When Jack...left, and I discovered I was pregnant and alone, Rob married me." Her voice broke. "He said he would have a part of me and Jack in you. I don't think he ever realized how much a part of *him* we all became because of his generosity."

"He was my friend in Vietnam." Jack stood to

pull a wallet out of his hip pocket. He pulled out a small folio of photographs and handed it to her. "We were stationed at Bienhoa, and Charlie was giving us a lot of trouble after the Tet offensive. Rob was down with a fever one day when our unit went out on patrol."

A brick lay on Kathy's lungs, preventing her from drawing anything but very shallow breaths. She looked through the photos with fingers that were beginning to shake. Two painfully young men in military fatigues, arms over each other's shoulders, wide smiles belying the horrors that must have existed in the jungle vegetation that surrounded them.

One she recognized instantly as a much younger version of her father. Or the man she'd always thought of as her father. The other was Jack, minus about thirty years.

"We were attacked, and half the guys got away, three died, and I was taken prisoner." He shook his head and drew a deep breath. His eyes lost focus, and Kathy concluded that the pictures in his mind must be terrible. "I saw and endured a lot of things over eighteen months that I thought I'd learned to live with after I got home. But...it was harder than I thought. Pictures, sounds..." He paused and closed his eyes as though trying to dispel the intrusion of those things right now. "They made it difficult to hold a job, to be with anyone. I tried both. That was when Rob and I worked at the print shop with your mom." He clutched her mother's hand. "But dedication and love require that you share, and I was living with images I couldn't in all conscience put anyone else through, much less someone I loved." He smiled thinly. "That story about the guy with the gun in the print shop was true, you know. It's just that Rob and I were under the table and we both pulled your mother under with us when she walked in the back door."

Kathy looked up at him, her brain functioning weakly.

"Anyway," he went on as though realizing that wasn't important at the moment. "Rob didn't have any family and my mom had died while I was in Nam, so your mother became our family. The three of us spent all our time together." He rubbed Patsy's hand with his free one, hesitating, clearing his throat. "But it was more than friendship for your mom and me. Unfortunately she discovered she was pregnant at the same time that I began to realize I couldn't live with what was in my head. It all came back to me in such ugly detail that I didn't think I could inflict it on her, so I left before she even had a chance to tell me about you."

Kathy found it difficult to swallow around the brick. It was going to choke her in a minute, she was sure of it, but this was about who she was and she had to listen.

"I spent a couple of years seeing therapists, and old friends of mine gave me jobs in construction. When I finally felt that I could look up your mom again, she was married to Rob. So I stayed away. Then, quite by accident a couple of years ago, I ran into someone we'd both known in those days, and she told me Rob had died and that Patsy was now running the print shop.

"She had a picture of you and your mother posed in front of the shop."

Kathy remembered vividly the day it had been

taken. Her father...Robert McQuade...had been gone only a few months, and she'd still been feeling terrified and cheated. But her mother had convinced her that they would manage just fine if they did it together, and her grief had gradually turned to commitment to help her mother through and to find her own courage.

She looked small and thin in the photograph, but she remembered how big she felt inside as they stood before the print shop sign.

"The minute I looked at your face," Jack said, his voice ragged and tight. "I knew you were mine."

For the first time since Jack had begun speaking, Kathy looked up into his eyes. They were miserable, hopeful, in pain.

"So I came back," he went on, "intent on claiming you as mine." His brow furrowed and his bottom lip began to tremble. "But I saw the strong and beautiful young woman you'd become, and knew the haunted wreck I'd always be inside and...I couldn't do it. So I stayed, just to be around the two of you."

He stopped again and swiped a hand across his eyes. Her mother was crying freely.

"Then something happened that I would never have thought could happen," he went on. "All the ugly images began to clear out of my head."

Kathy stared at him, waiting for him to explain. She felt dampness on her hands and realized it was her own tears.

"It was you," he said. "Pictures of you in my head started to crowd out everything else. I made up a past for us in my mind—me pushing you on a swing, taking you for an ice cream, driving you to school. You were so beautiful, so bright, so sure of who you were.'' He had to take another deep breath to go on. ''And who you were, was a part of me. Me! And your mother.'' He smiled suddenly. ''And like a miracle, I was better. But I had to make sure my recovery would last, so I had to go away for a while, to see how I would function on my own. My friend working construction was building a hospital in Maine, and he put me on the payroll. Your mother gave me her car and money to live for a couple of months and her blessing. I asked your mother not to tell you who I was, on the chance that it didn't work.''

''I didn't know what else to do,'' Patsy said, with tears in her eyes. ''So I let you believe what you wanted to believe. He brought back everything I'd lent him, Kathy. And more.'' She smiled through her tears at Jack. ''She was very upset because she thought you'd stolen cash from me, despite all my assurances that you hadn't.''

Jack smiled, too, then swiped at his eyes with the heel of his hand. ''Makes sense to me. Anyway, it worked, Kathy. I don't feel as though there's a black hole inside me anymore. But then you were becoming this...public phenomenon and I thought maybe the best thing to do was to stay away, at least until your tour was over, and your mother and I could talk and decide what was best for you.'' His shoulders stiffened and he wrapped an arm around Patsy. ''Then that reporter broadsided you on television, and I had to come and see what I could do.''

Kathy stared at her mother and Jack...at her *parents*...and all she could think about was how upset she'd been earlier in the day when she'd thought her mother hadn't trusted her enough to tell her the truth about herself. And how utterly unimportant that seemed now in light of what Jack must have suffered, of what her mother must have been through, loving a man unable to share himself with her because the memories he owned were too ugly, too painful, of what Rob had given for the love of his friends and their child.

She got to her feet and was aware of Gib standing with her as though prepared to support her—or catch her.

Her mother and Jack stood, too, her mother's expression anxious and desperate, Jack's clouded with all he'd been through. Under it, though, Kathy caught a glimpse of that particular adoration of father for daughter that she used to recognize in Robert McQuade's eyes even when she was just a little girl. It used to make her feel precious—and invincible.

And suddenly this chaotic day wasn't about all that had been kept from her, but rather all that had been given to her. And she had to react in kind.

Kathy went to her mother and Jack with arms outstretched, wrapping one around her mother's shoulders as she came toward her with a sob, and the other around Jack's waist as he stared at her in complete disbelief.

Then she felt him squeeze her to him and almost lost consciousness in the resulting three-way embrace.

GIB MADE MORE COFFEE. He remembered reading once that when women were confronted with a situation they couldn't handle, they cooked because it allowed them to make a familiar and welcome contribution.

Granted, it had probably been an old book analyzing women from a previous generation, but he found himself relating to it. He couldn't cook, but he *could* make coffee.

And if that weeping, laughing reunion in the living room was trying to tell him that love truly *did* exist and that it could survive hellish experiences and distance and interruption and deception, then he didn't want to hear it.

He'd been willing to admit to himself that he loved Kathy because she was unique and beautiful and she really knew nothing about love herself—and therefore couldn't expect more from him than he could give her.

But Jack's and Patsy's revelation had put a new complexion on it, and he suspected he was out of his league.

Jack Trent, clearly tortured by war memories, had still managed to hold his love for Patsy, then, when he found out about Kathy, his love for her, as well. And finally, a challenge to their safety—at least emotionally—had led him to take his fears in hand and run to their defense.

Patsy had borne an enormous and painful burden all alone, living on the blind faith that her love would one day reunite her family.

And Kathy, whom he'd always thought lived with one foot in a dreamworld, accepted the truth with generosity and an open heart, apparently oblivious to or uncaring of the fact that this might put an end to her brief career as an author and darling of the media.

He couldn't love like that. He hadn't the experience. He hadn't the genes.

He found two one ounce-size bottles of brandy in the courtesy bar and put a half ounce in each cup of coffee. Then he carried them back into the living room.

Everyone still looked a little stunned, but they were more relaxed, and Kathy seemed to have the situation in hand. She was now sitting between Jack and Patsy on the sofa.

"I promised to talk to the press," Patsy said gravely. "I'll just explain everything."

Kathy shook her head. "I don't see why we should have to explain anything."

"Someone has to explain," Jack said. "I think it should be me."

Gib interrupted the argument with a quiet "If I may interrupt?"

Patsy smiled warmly at him. "Of course, dear."

"I think Kathy will be expected to explain. I can put word out tonight that she'll hold a press conference in the morning. Our flight to Phoenix doesn't leave until two in the afternoon. I think she should be honest and reveal whatever you all agree upon. She seems to have a way of putting things that seduces the press. I think they'll be as fair with her as the general sordid quality of muckraking will allow, then how the public accepts it will be entirely up to them. And, ultimately, of course, that will determine whether this tour was a boon or a bust. After Phoenix, there's just Reno and L.A., then we're on our way home."

Kathy looked suddenly very tired and leaned back

against the cushions with her coffee. "How do you think they'll react?" she asked Gib.

He shrugged a shoulder noncommittally. "Hard to tell. The romantics, of course, will eat it up. War hero reunites with loving family. But there are a lot of skeptics out there, too."

Her eyes met his and he knew with certainty that she was reading his mind. He was one of the skeptics. If he hadn't been personally involved in all this, he wouldn't believe it, either.

She took a sip of her coffee. A slight widening of her eyes indicated she'd noticed the brandy, then she held the cup serenely in her lap and skewered him with a quiet but demanding look. "You think the tour will ultimately be a bust?"

He held her gaze and shook his head. "Not at all. I think you will endure. People love you and believe in you."

"And which are you? Romantic or skeptic?"

He was not going to have this out now. "Bodyguards maintain a certain neutrality," he said easily. "The job requires it. So we're in agreement about the conference?"

Patsy and Jack nodded.

Kathy resisted for a moment, searching Gib's eyes, looking into his for some sign that she was wrong about what she was seeing there.

He didn't give it to her.

"All right," she said finally. "But I do all the talking."

"Don't you always?" Patsy asked.

GIB HAD EXPECTED a confrontation, but he hadn't expected Kathy to stage it in the middle of the night in his room. Jack was sleeping in Patsy's.

Gib was lying on top of the covers in the dark in the slacks and sweater he'd worn all day and his stocking feet. At the sound of his doorknob turning, he lay absolutely still, praying that it was an intruder and not Kathy.

But his prayer went unanswered. Kathy's fresh, wildflower scent wafted in ahead of her.

Gib lay absolutely still, hoping to convince her that he was asleep and to discourage the discussion he was sure she had in mind. He thought he might be succeeding when she didn't turn on the light.

Then his heart sank, though it began to beat wildly as he sensed rather than heard her quiet advance on the carpeted floor. He felt the mattress on the other side of the bed take her weight. He remained determinedly still, afraid even to breathe.

A hand smacked him lightly right in the middle of his chest. "Come on," she said, keeping her voice down. "I know you're a better bodyguard than this. If you really had been asleep, you'd have wakened the minute I turned the doorknob, and you'd have me in a headlock at this very moment."

"That's a tempting picture." Resigned to the inevitable, he reached an arm out to turn on the bedside table lamp.

She sat up right beside him, her hip resting against the side of his waist, her legs tucked under her. She still wore her sweats, and her hair was caught loosely at the nape of her neck with a ruffly thing. Her face was completely devoid of makeup, and her freckles softened the shadows cast on her by the small pool of light. She looked pale and just a little...different.

She leaned sideways so that she could rest her forearm on the jut of his ribs. "It only *seems* like a tempting picture because you don't want to have to deal with it," she said with a soft smile, "but if you really gave it some thought, what would you do without me?"

He had no idea. He couldn't conceive of day-to-day survival, much less having any hope for an old age. But life without her was precisely his fate.

"Oh, let me think," he said, pretending to frown as he stared at the ceiling. "No carrying eighty pounds of luggage, no fighting my way through reporters, no wimpy coffee, no chasing you through strange cities, no one countermanding my every decision. Whatever would I do with my time?"

She blew air between her lips in a very unladylike way that melted his heart to syrup. "You're a soldier, Gib, even in your everyday life. You'd wither away if it was ever that easy for you."

"I'm reckless enough to want to try it."

She accepted that reply without an answering sally and straightened. He was about to congratulate himself on talking her out of this argument when she simply repositioned herself, propped the pillows up against the headboard on the free side of the bed and sat against them.

God. She was only changing strategies.

"This afternoon," she said, crossing her ankles, "you said you were falling in love with me."

"No, I didn't," he disputed. "I said..."

"Okay, be technical. You said you were beginning to believe in love. But you meant, because you were falling in love with me."

"You're sure about that?"

"Quite."

Maybe brutal honesty was the only way to deal with this. He sat up against his own pillows and stared at the door as she was doing. "Okay, I am in love with you. But that doesn't mean I'm going to let anything come of it."

She rolled her head against the headboard and blinked in surprise. "Do you think you can stop it?"

He folded his arms, ignoring the sudden rush of emotion he felt at the sight of her ivory face on a pillow beside him. He'd dreamed this very picture.

"Of course I can. You're the one who's always telling kids that their brains can overpower their bodies."

She sat up a little higher. "Okay, but I'm not talking about doing something sexual about it, I'm talking about stopping love from simply being. Love has roots, Gib. And skis and wheels and tracks and—" She stopped, and her voice dropped a decibel. "It can fly, Gib. I hate to be the one to tell you this, but I don't think you can escape it."

Gib shifted to sit cross-legged, facing her. He spoke quietly, but put on his most severe face. "Kathy, listen to me," he demanded. "This is the first time you've ever found yourself in love, and you think that because it seems like such a wonderful thing, it *has* to be yours. But I'm telling you that you can't have it with *me*."

She looked at him as though he was insane. "Well, pardon me, but you don't just go out and pick someone to be in love with. It comes to you. Like a gift."

Gib shook his head at her. "Kathy, love with me would not be a gift. I'd be like a boxful of nothing.

I've never had it, wouldn't know what to do with it, don't know how to give it back."

"I'm sure that comes with the doing, Gib."

"Providing you have something to work with."

She stared at him a moment, her eyes disbelieving, then without warning, she grabbed the hem of her sweatshirt and began to pull it off. He was momentarily distracted by the sight of her small, round breasts cupped in lacy pink silk, then pulled himself together and tugged down on the fabric in her hands.

"What do you—" He remembered her mother and Jack and whispered harshly instead, "What do you think you're doing?"

"I love you," she insisted, wrestling him for the hem of her shirt, "and if I can't make you understand that on my terms, then I'll have to do it on yours. Now let go. We're not going to be able to make love with me dressed."

"Kathy!"

She yanked backward, trying to evade his fingers, and fell onto the pillow. The shirt was now all the way up her arms and almost off, and he'd fallen on top of her.

Her naked skin touched his hands, his cheek, his throat. To avoid touching her, he held his arms out and away from her as though he were in a freefall. It occurred to him that that was an astonishingly appropriate metaphor.

He pushed himself to his knees astride her, caught her hands before she could pull the shirt off them, and scooped her up against him in one arm until she, too, was on her knees. Then he freed her hands and struggled to yank the shirt back down.

But she was leaning into him, combing her fingers

through his hair, the wildflower garden of her fragrance snaking around him as she nibbled at his earlobe.

"Don't be afraid, Gib," she whispered in his ear. He felt the tip of her tongue dip inside. "I'm trying to show you that you have love to give. You refuse to see it my way because with you everything has to have a physical definition. You don't believe in the heart. All right. I'm trying to accept that. Let's make love, and I'll show you what I mean."

He yanked her shirt down with a gesture so firm she felt as though she sank three inches into the mattress.

"What?" she asked, pretending innocence.

"You are not showing me anything! You still have two cities and five days left on the tour!"

She nodded knowingly, enjoying his mounting distress. This was precisely the reaction she'd hoped for. "I don't care about the tour."

"Well, I care about the tour! You get up in front of that press conference tomorrow with a smirk on your face and it's all over for all of us!"

She smirked anyway. "You really think you can make me smile?"

"Guaranteed."

She started pulling on the shirt again. "Well, then, let's—"

"Stop it!" He shook her. "I know it's Jurassic of me, but I am *not* taking a virgin."

"You're not taking anything, I'm offering—"

He put a hand over her mouth, backed off the bed and with an arm around her waist pulled her with him until he could lift her off the bed and onto her feet.

He pointed to the door. "Go back to your room," he advised, "and go to sleep."

She remained where he'd placed her and pretended puzzlement. "Well, I don't understand this. I try to give myself to you, but you won't take me. What do you suppose is preventing you from indulging a lifelong creed of sex without emotional attachment?"

She saw the desperation in him and was not surprised when he lowered his face to hers and said coolly, "Perhaps it's that you just don't appeal to me."

She grinned. "Gib. We just rolled around together on the bed, and I'm aware of evidence to the contrary."

His eyes darkening, he caught her arm and walked her to the door.

"Could it be," she asked quickly, realizing she didn't have much time, "that you're coming to understand how I feel and even if you can't quite agree with me, you want me to be able to have it my way?"

He opened the door without answering.

"What could you be feeling for me that would make you place my feelings above yours, even when I'm trying to give you what *you* want?"

He pushed her out into the hallway.

"Love, that's what!" she whispered loudly. "You're feeling love!"

His door closed in her face.

Chapter Eleven

Kathy beamed her way through the press conference. In the wee hours of the morning, while she'd been curled up in the fetal position in the middle of the hotel's king-size bed, wondering what Gib was thinking and doing, she'd realized that however things worked out for her personally, her mother had found happiness.

And Kathy had found her father.

Robert McQuade would also always be her father because she felt as though she were half composed of his loving kindness and his careful practicality. She would simply be one of those rare people lucky enough to have been doubly loved.

A spark of heady satisfaction was lit inside her that nothing could extinguish.

But she wanted Gib. Oh, how she wanted Gib! The fact that he wouldn't let her make love to him last night proved to her that he cared more than he ever had about any other woman. Proved that his denials were absurd and he did have love to give.

She wanted to think that when he'd pushed her out into the hall last night and closed the door on her, he was loving her.

But this morning he'd been setting up the press conference when she'd arrived, then he'd introduced her to the station manager of KDVX, who'd come by personally to apologize for Max Blaine's attack on her and to assure her that he'd gone ahead with that line of questioning without the station's approval.

Then the *Denver Post* had wanted to photograph the two of them together, then her with her parents, then it was time for the conference to begin.

Gib was keeping his distance, and she knew she had no choice but to let him have it. But the moment this tour was over…

Jack and her mother had told her to tell the press everything, and she did. She admitted that the news had been a shock, but that she found it exciting to have her father in her life.

"What about Gib London?" a female reporter shouted from the back of the room. "Does he still fit in all this?"

"Yes!" Patsy replied. "Jack and I want him for a son-in-law."

Everyone laughed. Gib, standing near the door, waved goodnaturedly as strobe lights went off in his direction.

"Is that in your future?" someone else wanted to know of Kathy. "Or should we look for Representative Neil Barton?"

Kathy raised her hands to express uncertainty. "Romance requires your full attention," she said, "and since this tour began I've been a little too busy to think about anything else." And then a little devil prodded her to add, "Neil is planning to meet us in

Phoenix for a day or two. You'll have to talk to him."

Gib shifted his weight, otherwise Kathy noted no reaction in him at that suggestion. She tried not to look disappointed.

"How do you think it went?" Kathy asked Patsy as Jack and Gib followed them to the elevator after the conference.

Patsy hugged her fiercely. "You were wonderful. You amaze me. They seemed entirely in sympathy with you."

Jack patted Kathy's shoulder. "I can't believe how good you made us all look by telling them how important we are to you. Is that…true?"

"I haven't had a father since I was nine," she replied with a wistful smile. "I'm delighted to have found you. And though I still don't really know you as a dad, you're important to Mom, and she's very important to me."

"They seemed accepting," Gib said, feeling called upon to be the voice of reality here, "but we won't really know how they choose to present the story until the afternoon news. I imagine Phoenix will pick it up since we're on our way there."

He pretended not to notice Kathy's glance in his direction when her parents stepped out of the elevator together and started down the hall to their room.

He still hadn't recovered from last night and didn't expect to for some time.

He wanted to be relieved that Kathy had told the press Barton was still in the running, because it relieved him of the responsibility of having to produce a love worthy of hers.

But Gib suspected that either she'd said that simply to get a reaction from him or that she was indeed still ambivalent about Barton, in which case he might be forced to save her from herself.

So it didn't help his personal dilemma. Not at all.

THE USUAL LIMOUSINE met Kathy and her party at the airport—but so did a crowd of about a hundred people carrying signs.

As Gib, Kathy and her parents, with their luggage piled onto a cart, headed for the terminal doors, Gib stopped abruptly, flinging an arm out to stop Kathy.

"What?" she asked.

He pointed to the group mingling formlessly beyond the double glass doors.

"You think they're…waiting for me?"

"Yeah. I can't read all the signs from here, but one of them has your name on it."

"You think they're hostile?" Patsy asked anxiously.

"I don't know," Gib replied. "We haven't heard a news report yet. It's hard to predict a public reaction to something like that. But our limo's out there, so we have to go through them." He turned to Jack. "I'll come back for the bags. We just move fast without stopping and get them in the limo. All right?"

Jack put an arm around Patsy's shoulders. "All right."

Gib then looked from Kathy to Patsy. "Even if they're friendly, we keep moving until we're in the limo. A crowd, even one that likes you, has the potential to be trouble."

Firmly tucked into the curve of his arm, Kathy

asked quietly, "Does that mean we can consider *you* a crowd?"

He pinched her upper arm. "Just keep walking."

The moment Gib and Kathy cleared the door, the greeters turned toward them, shouting. Kathy felt a cold stab of fear, grateful for Gib's tall, solid presence nearly wrapped around her.

Then she realized that the shouts were cheers of encouragement, and smiles and supportive slogans were offered as the group followed them to the limo.

"We're with you, Kathy!"

"Virgins for Kathy McQuade!"

"Way to go Jack!"

"Gib loves Kathy!"

"The Phoenix Youth for Celibacy Coalition supports Kathy McQuade!"

The limousine driver opened the back door and helped hold the crowd back while Gib saw Kathy and her parents in.

Kathy blew kisses and waved through the window while Gib went back for the bags. He and the driver packed them into the trunk.

Then Gib, walking back around the car, was grabbed by a rotund older woman. She seemed to be delivering a sermon of some kind, the shake of her index finger adding gravity to her words. Gib hugged her in return, then climbed into the car.

"What did she say to you?" Patsy wanted to know as he resumed his seat beside Kathy.

He smiled. "Just some good motherly advice." He turned toward the driver. "You can go now, Wally."

"The news must have been favorable," Patsy observed as they drove off.

Kathy glanced at her watch. "We'll see for ourselves. We should get to the hotel in plenty of time to catch the news."

THERE WAS A LARGE BASKET of flowers awaiting Kathy on the sofa table in the hotel room. Her parents went immediately toward the large double doors that led out onto a garden of succulents. Gib went to check the bedrooms—a habit since Kathy's closet incident in Denver.

Kathy leaned close to the sweet-smelling stargazer lilies and roses, and all the other beautiful flowers that made up the giant arrangement. It was rejuvenating just to take in the fragrance.

She took the tiny envelope from its holder and pulled out the card.

"Hi, Kathy!" it read. "Something came up in budget committee at the last minute, and I can't join you in Phoenix. Can't tell at this point when I'll be free, but hope it's soon. Hope you're still having fun. Neil."

Kathy stood with the card in hand, the fragrance of the flowers surrounding her, the sight of her parents, arm in arm, inspecting the garden, and thought it fortunate that she didn't have serious feelings for Neil.

She'd been flattered by his attentions and somewhat enjoyed the jealousy Gib tried hard to conceal every time she mentioned Neil. But her attentions had never been seriously engaged. What she felt for Gib made that very clear.

Still, she was surprised to discover that Gib had been right about him. She knew this note was not about a sudden problem in the budget committee. It meant he'd heard the news about her parents, and he didn't want to be seen with Kathy until public opinion had been clearly defined.

So, here I am, she thought a little grimly. Probably destined to be a virgin for all eternity. The man who professed publicly to loving me is waiting out the mood of my former fans to determine whether or not he really does. And the man I love can't or won't love me.

Great.

She tried to put a positive spin on it. It would be easy to write fiction now because there would be no distractions.

If Kathy's romantic life was in shambles, her life as an author and virginity guru was an astounding success.

The afternoon news and all news coverage for the next few days had segments from her Denver press conference, then from her welcome at the Phoenix airport. One commentator said she considered Kathy proof that values—old or new—could be the guiding force of a life, without making that person ridiculous.

"She isn't sappy or sanctimonious or judgmental. She's just real and focused. And she's waiting for a man who appreciates that. Go, Kathy." The reporter smiled, then added, as though warning all men, "And nobody gets nothin' until she finds him."

Well-wishers collected outside the hotel when she came and went for interviews and appearances. The hotel suite was filled with their gifts of flowers and balloons. The hotel staff from the manager to the busboys in the restaurant called to her as she passed.

She stood alone in the small garden the night after

her last interview in Phoenix. In the morning they would be leaving for Reno. The moon was large and bright, the breeze soft and cool.

She turned at the sound of a footstep on the brick walk, her heart picking up its beat. But it was Jack and not Gib.

He came to stand beside her and look up at the sky.

"The fact that I came home with any sanity at all," he said softly, "is thanks to that sky. I'd look up at it through the bars in an alien landscape populated by brutal people, and it was the only thing that was familiar—the one thing in my whole memory that was like anything I'd known before. The sky. The stars. But for a long time, it still wasn't enough to help me go forward."

He sighed. Kathy listened. She was trying hard to connect with him, but her life was such a chaotic tangle at the moment. He and Gib seemed to be becoming friends with a lot to say to each other and a lot to laugh about. She knew their war experiences, though very different, had forged a bond between them.

But she was still finding her way—with both of them.

"When I came back to Bayside," he went on slowly, as though with difficulty, "discovering that your mother still loved me after all that time helped me start to shape a place for myself again. And just knowing you were a part of me gave me a renewed sense of myself because you were so...amazing."

Amazing. Kathy said the word over to herself. Even in the midst of all the attention the media and the public were giving her, hearing herself referred to as amazing was nothing short of...amazing.

"But when I went away and began to discover that I was definitely better, I wasn't sure I could fit into your life. Then I saw you in that interview with Max Blaine, and I saw him deliberately try to hurt you and I felt such anger, such protective fury because I wasn't there to shield you, that I suddenly had no doubt about it."

He stood with his hands in his pockets, and Kathy looped her arm in his.

"I was very much alive," he went on with a small laugh. "Very much in place in the world—at least as a father. You gave me that, you know. You brought me back."

She looked up at him guiltily. "But I was rude to you before I understood..."

He negated that with a shake of his head. "Didn't matter. I knew I was your father and you were my daughter." Then with another laugh he took the hand she'd tucked into his arm and brought it to his lips. "Of course, this is much better. Now, what are you going to do about Gib?"

She frowned teasingly. "You don't think that gives you the right to interfere, do you? Mom tries that, too, and I don't let her get away with it, either." Then she grew serious. "Gib was a very rich and very neglected child, and learned to get by by turning off all that cozy family stuff and staying disconnected from everyone. He grew up knowing love didn't exist for him, and chose to be with women who verified that for him. Apparently he's had lots of sex but no love."

"You're going to correct him on that. Right?"

Kathy frowned into the moonlight. "I thought I could. Now I'm not so sure. Can you change a pattern that's woven into a life that way?"

He put an arm around her shoulders to hold her close and laughed lightly. "Your mom just sort of...embroidered over my old patterns. And you're half her, you know."

THE CROWD at the Reno Airport was twice the size of the group that had met Kathy in Phoenix. They raised first and second fingers into the air in the sign of a *V* and chanted "Virgin! Virgin!" over and over.

"I hate being protected from love and affection," Kathy protested as Gib hustled her from the airport terminal to yet another waiting limo. "Theirs *or* yours."

"Now is not the time," he replied without missing a step.

A man moved into their path, and Gib held Kathy close and put an arm out, prepared to fling him aside.

But the man shouted, "Kathy! Darling!" It was Neil. And he was in the company of a man who introduced himself to Gib and Kathy as the mayor of Reno.

"Please," the mayor said to Gib. "We've prepared a small welcome for Kathy, and I do have officers watching the crowd. Will you let me take her to the microphone we've set up?"

Gib looked around, spotted several police officers on the fringe of the crowd and several interspersed with them.

"All right," he replied. "But I'm staying with her."

"Of course." The mayor extended his hand to Jack. "Jack Trent?"

Jack shook his hand. "Yes."

The mayor clasped his hand in both of his. "I lost a brother in Da Nang. Glad to have you here. Come and join us."

Gib watched as Neil hung on Kathy now that he was sure she had the crowd's affection and approval. Kathy hadn't said anything about the note that had accompanied the flowers Neil had sent to the Phoenix hotel room, but her mother had shown it to him.

To Kathy's credit, she didn't seem to be paying much attention to Neil while she spoke to the crowd, but Gib would have liked it better if she'd handled him the same way she'd taken care of the Armani ad in the New Orleans jazz club.

But the increased news and crowd attention had made her even more gracious in public, more courteous, more considerate of everyone involved with her.

The mayor presented her with a key to the city, then extended a special invitation to her and her family to join him and the city council and their wives at a dinner in honor of Kathy and her family at The Royal Reno.

The mayor promised Gib that the police chief and the commissioner would be there if he wanted a night off.

"Why don't you take the night off?" Kathy asked at the hotel. This suite was like something out of ancient Egypt and made him feel as though he'd been entombed with his entire entourage but someone else's earthly goods.

"No," he said, checking out the coffeemaker.

This place had a small corridor kitchen, sandwiched in between the entry hall and one of the bedrooms. "This isn't the kind of job you hand off to someone else."

She leaned a shoulder in the doorway and watched him as he sorted through the packets of coffee left in a small wicker basket on the counter. "Well, I hope you don't intend to be a pervasive, demoralizing force tonight, because I have business to take care of."

He looked up, surprised and suspicious. "What kind of business?"

"Personal."

"With Neil?"

"Yes."

A dozen warnings came to mind, but as she was always reminding him—though she was a virgin, she was old enough to know her own mind. And she certainly seemed to.

"Just stay in sight," he said. "And don't let him get too amorous or I may have to hit him on general principle."

"Because you're jealous?"

"Because he's a jerk."

"But you *are* jealous?"

He pretended to think about that. Actually, *jealous* didn't begin to describe what he felt. He sniffed the only packet of unflavored coffee in the lot.

"I think I'm more offended that you can claim to be interested in me," he said evenly, pulling open the foil packet, "and interested in him at the same time, when we're as different as night and day."

She walked into the kitchen to open the courtesy refrigerator. "You're not that different. He's afraid of having to do anything for himself in a physical sense, so he allies himself with people who'll advance his plan.'' She pulled out a can of nuts and closed the door. She smiled at him amiably as she caught her index finger in the ring on the lid and pulled it off. A whoosh of air filled the small space. ''You're afraid of having to do anything in an emotional sense, and you use only women who require nothing from you. Basically, the same principle.''

He knew this was a deliberate plot to provoke him. He focused his attention on filling the coffee carafe with water, privately pleased to hear that she finally seemed to have Barton pegged.

''Hardly the same thing,'' he argued. ''The women in my life know what to expect.''

''Anything but love?''

Her candor was beginning to exhaust him. He completed the coffee-making ritual, turned the pot on, then folded his arms and leaned back against the counter, meeting her gaze. It was wide-eyed and innocently interested, but after almost a month he could read her like a book. Books were his business, after all.

''I thought we'd been through all this,'' he said.

She came to lean beside him, popping a macadamia nut into her mouth. She chewed and offered the can to him. ''We have, but I thought you and I might be in a different situation. You admitted you loved me, remember? We sat side by side in your bed and you told me you loved me. Doesn't that change anything?'' Her voice rose a little in agitation, belying the casual pose she presented. ''How can that not change anything?''

He took the can of nuts from her and put them on

the counter. "It can't change anything, because the fact remains that though I feel love, I don't know how to give it. And look at the love you've experienced in your life. Robert, who loved your mother and his friend so much that he married her and became your father so completely. Then your own father, who's been kept alive and functioning—despite horrible memories—by his love for your mother and for you and for the friend who stepped in to do what he couldn't."

Her eyes brimmed with tears at that summation of the first twenty-six years of her life. "I know. But that just makes *me* overflow with love."

He nodded. "And that's my point. With that history, do you really think you can spend the rest of your life with someone who doesn't know how it's done?"

She growled and rolled her eyes at him. "Gib, it's just done day by day. And I imagine the more you do it, the better you get at it. I promise you if you have trouble loving me, I'll have enough to carry us through."

Kathy saw she was making no impression on him. The knowledge came to her like a cold certainty in the pit of her stomach.

"I don't want that for you," he said gravely, taking a gentle hold on her upper arm. "I want you to have everything you've been waiting for."

Everything she'd been waiting for.

Kathy didn't usually consider the cost of waiting for the man who she was so sure waited for *her*. But the fact that he was here and wouldn't admit it made her remember every lonely moment, every scornful smirk from amorous men who couldn't believe she was serious when she said no, every need within herself that sometimes rose to question her decision.

And that cold reality in the pit of her stomach became something very hot, something that began to spark.

She yanked her arm out of his grasp angrily. "Oh, don't try to tell me you're doing this for me!" she shouted at him. When he shushed her, she lowered her voice to a harsh whisper. "You're protecting yourself, not me! Some welcher you are! My bodyguard turns out to be the only one who can really hurt me."

She started to walk away, but he caught her arm. His hazel eyes were as turbulent as she felt. "I explained my position in the beginning," he said defensively but quietly.

"Yes, you did," she granted him, "but your position changed, didn't it? You now love me. The rest of you just can't go along with it."

"Kathy..."

She was on the brink of hysterical tears, but she swallowed hard and became suddenly very calm. "Don't worry about it." She gently removed his hand from her. "Actually, this has clarified a lot of things for me. I see everything in a new light. I was naive."

"Come on," he chided, frowning. "You've got an entire country full of young women believing—"

"Not about celibacy," she interrupted, knowing he misread her. "I'm right about that. It's safe and sensible. It was thinking that I'd finally be able to put it aside with a man I loved and who would love me. The truth is that after all that care and patience, I still have to settle, just like everyone else does."

"You're not talking about Barton?" he asked grimly.

She was now so cool and calm she was almost frightening herself. "Yes, I am. When you're filled with love, you have to give, and he'll let me do that. You won't."

His eyes darkened. "Kathy," he said in a strangled whisper. "Giving love to him would be like throwing it down the drain."

She shrugged a shoulder. "Giving it to you, is having it thrown back in my face. Hardly an improvement."

"Then wait for somebody else!"

That almost renewed her temper, but she was feeling so much stronger when she controlled it. So she drew a breath. "I'm tired of waiting, Gib. I want a real life now, and children. Children..." She almost lost it there. Controlling her emotions was much harder than controlling her temper. "Children know how to accept love and how to give it back. Excuse me. I have to get ready."

Chapter Twelve

Kathy was beginning to give serious thought to life in the convent.

She had no intention of marrying Neil Barton, but she also had no intention of letting Gib London know that she hadn't a clue what to do about her future. She *was* tired of waiting, and she *did* long for children, but there were now thousands, possibly millions, of young women across the country aware of her every move. And she couldn't let them down.

Most important, after all she'd endured in the process of this book and this tour, she wouldn't let herself down. She had to live with herself for the next fifty or sixty years.

She now sat with Neil in the back of the limousine that was taking them to the mayor's party. Gib sat in the front with the driver behind the privacy shield, his only concession to allowing them time alone.

The mayor had picked up Jack and Patsy himself.

Gib looked absolutely gorgeous in a dark suit and tie, but Kathy had made a point of failing to notice.

Neil also looked elegant in a less-dangerous and more blueblood sort of way. And he was more determinedly charming than usual tonight. He'd come to the hotel bearing flowers and chocolates and had kept up a witty patter since they'd climbed into the limo.

Kathy was finding it difficult to get a word in edgewise.

"...and I think it's time we give the press what they've been waiting for," he said.

Kathy raised a questioning eyebrow. "What have they been waiting for?"

"The announcement of our engagement," he replied, as though that should have been clear to a child. "Don't tell me you haven't noticed. They're waiting for the virgin princess to announce her betrothal to the lord of the land. Or in this case—" he dipped his head in an attempt at modesty that didn't quite come off "—the United States senator."

It was all she could do not to groan aloud. "Neil, you're a state representative."

The arm around her shoulders tightened. "But not for long. Allied with you, I could become president."

Perversely she said, "I thought the press seemed rather interested in Gib London and me."

Neil made a scornful sound. "The tabs, maybe. I think they like the idea of the virgin and the bodyguard for its illicit appeal."

"Illicit?" she asked in surprise.

But they had reached their destination, and a liveried doorman came to let Neil out of the back of the limo. He turned to help Kathy. Reporters immediately swamped them.

Gib held them at bay with the doorman's assistance. Neil hurried her into the elegant hotel where someone on staff already had an elevator waiting. ‘‘The dining room’s on the top floor,’’ he told Neil.

Neil thanked him as he ushered Kathy inside.

Gib followed, but was stopped abruptly by the sound of his name being called from the lobby. Kathy watched him turn as his three aunts hurried toward him, arms extended.

In the moment he hesitated, Neil pushed the Close door button, and the elevator began to ascend.

GIB DIDN’T KNOW which he was most annoyed about—losing sight of Kathy when she was with Barton, or the completely unexpected sight of his aunts in Reno, Nevada.

But they clustered around him, rose and lavender hugs driving away all annoyance. Still, he didn’t like the idea of Kathy being out of sight.

He glanced at the elevator doors as the mayor approached them with Patsy and Jack, then turned back to his aunts, his arms around Rose and Lucinda, Cordelia pinched into the middle of them. ‘‘What are you doing here?’’ he asked. ‘‘Is everything all right?’’

‘‘That’s what we wondered,’’ Cordelia replied for them. ‘‘We’re fine, but are you all right? And Kathy?’’

Before he could answer, Lucinda said breathlessly, ‘‘We couldn’t get a room at your hotel, so we booked into this one. You were enroute and we couldn’t reach you.’’

‘‘When the desk clerk learned who we were,’’ Rose put in, ‘‘he told us the mayor had planned a party in Kathy’s honor. So we called and got invited.’’

"Wonderful," Gib said, shepherding them toward the elevator. "Well, let's go up to the dining room. I don't like Kathy being out of sight."

"Are you in love with her?" Rose asked hopefully. Cordelia and Lucinda waited.

The elevator doors parted as they approached and he followed his aunts onto the car. "Yes," he heard himself admit. "But...she has her eye on Barton."

Cordelia frowned at him as she drew him between her and Lucinda. "She has her heart on you. It's plain for all to see in every photo that's been taken of the two of you. What's this nonsense about Neil Barton?"

"She thinks she can be...happy with him." That wasn't at all what Kathy had said, and he diverted his lying gaze by pretending to study the illuminated floor numbers above the elevator doors.

After a moment Cordelia said, "Oh, I see. She thinks she can be happy with him, because you won't let her be happy with you."

"Well, of all the twitter-pated—" Rose dug in a small, antiquated, beaded bag hanging from her wrist and brought up a folded square of newsprint. "Have you looked at this?" she demanded, handing it to him. "Really looked at it."

Lucinda shook her head at Cordelia. "'Twitter-pated,'" she said in disgust. "The word went out with Jane Austen, and Rose is still using it."

Cordelia nodded. "It's better than 'moldy fig.'"

KATHY BEGAN TO SUSPECT Neil had a plan when he closed the door on Gib and pushed the seventh-floor button rather than the penthouse where the restaurant was located.

But she didn't question him when he led her off on seven, then to the room at the far end of the hall. He inserted his key in the lock. "This is where I'm staying," he said with the charming smile he'd been bestowing upon her all evening.

Kathy walked into the room, thinking that he had a lot to learn about subtlety, but she did need a little private time with him to tell him she wouldn't be seeing him anymore.

Neil gestured her to a blue-and-white, flower-patterned love seat and sat beside her. As she angled her body toward his to tell him what was on her mind, he wrapped an arm around her and kissed her. He was sloppy and overeager—and he wasn't Gib. She pushed him forcefully away.

He looked hurt and surprised. "What?" he asked, betraying annoyance for an instant, before covering it with a smile. "We're alone. No one's watching. And I'm going to announce our engagement at dinner."

She made no effort to hide *her* annoyance. "Neil, you're not."

"You're afraid you'll hold me back." He smiled beatifically upon her as though she should feel somehow blessed. "We've talked about it, Kathy. I know your background probably makes you uncomfortable with the idea of being married to a senator. But it's all right. We'll just keep your past quiet."

"My past?" she questioned in disbelief.

But he was on some internal high and didn't notice. "And since our engagement is imminent and no one knows where we are, I think this has finally gone on long enough."

"What's gone on long enough?"

He leaned into her, and she backed away, pushing against his chest. "This virginity thing," he said, putting a hand to her knee and rubbing his thumb across her thigh. "It's served its purpose, sweetheart. Your book made the *New York Times* bestseller list today, and my rating's up seven points. You go to L.A. day after tomorrow, then it's all over."

She couldn't believe her ears. She'd learned in Phoenix that Gib had been right about him, but she hadn't had any idea he'd been this right.

She now pushed against him in earnest. "You never *believed* what I wrote. Or anything I've said."

He straightened and laughed. "Kathy. What guy in his right mind *would* believe in celibacy? In conservative New England it's a vote-getter. That's all. But it's all right. I know *you* believe in it, and the voters will eat up the senatorial candidate having a virgin bride." His eyes focused suddenly on her lips, then wandered to the scooped neck of her cocktail dress with leering appreciation. When he looked back into her eyes again, his had narrowed. "But they only have to *think* that, Kathy. And we're as good as engaged. Let me introduce you to what you've saved yourself for all these years."

When she gasped, almost speechless with disgust, he added quickly, "Don't worry about the party. I told the mayor we might be missing for a little while."

Kathy shoved him for all she was worth and got to her feet. "You certainly *are* missing, Neil!" she shouted at him, snatching her purse up off the coffee table. "You're missing the point! The boat! Your marbles! Whatever in this world anyone could lack, you certainly do!"

He caught her arm, one knee still on the couch. He looked astonished. "Kathy, what is this emotional—"

"You two-faced liar!" she said, tugging on her arm. "Your voters only have to *think* I'm a virgin. What else do you promise them that they only have to *think* you'll deliver?"

"I cater to my voters!" he said with theatrical dignity.

"No, you don't!" she argued. "You cater to their vote! When Max Blaine ambushed me with the news about my parents, you decided *not* to meet me in Phoenix after all."

"I explained that! It was a budget committee meeting. But I'm here now!"

"Now that public opinion is on her side."

Both Kathy and Neil turned to the door as a new voice joined the argument. Gib walked into the room, an edge of anger in his movements, an air of readiness about him.

"Let her go," he said, a threat implied in the command.

Neil dropped his hand from her arm and got to his feet, his face filling with angry color. "How did you get in here?"

Gib held up a key. "I explained my concerns to the manager." He extended a hand to Kathy.

She took it, grateful for the sturdy strength in it. She'd have gotten out of this herself, but it was comforting to know he'd cared enough to find her.

Of course, she told herself unhappily. That's his job.

"The budget committee did not meet while we were in Phoenix," Gib said to Neil. "I had a friend in Boston call the Commonwealth's House of Representatives.'' When Kathy turned to him in surprise, he explained. ''On the chance that you were serious about him, I wanted to know whether or not he'd lied.'' He focused on Neil again. ''I think, considering everything, it would be best if you skipped the dinner. I'll tell the mayor you were called away.'' He smiled menacingly. ''To a budget committee meeting.''

''What are you going to tell the press?'' Neil asked a little plaintively as Gib led Kathy to the door.

''Nothing,'' Gib replied. ''Providing you leave Kathy's name out of any announcements from now on—public or personal.''

He led Kathy out into the hallway and pulled the door closed behind him. He took her chin between his thumb and forefinger and looked into her eyes. ''You all right?'' he asked, as though expecting her to be upset about discovering the real Neil.

She nodded. ''I'm fine. Thank you. I didn't know he intended to evade you like that.''

The cool ruthlessness left him suddenly. Now he was angry as he pulled her with him toward the elevators. ''I can't believe you let him take you into a hotel room. Your knee to the groin isn't going to work in every situation, you know. He had a hundred pounds on you. Don't you have any instincts for self-preservation?''

She drew her hand out of his, because the comfort it offered despite his words was only torturing her. ''I'm developing one,'' she said, and moved onto an elevator as the doors opened.

GIB EXPLAINED Neil's sudden absence to the mayor and the council members as smoothly as he'd promised he would, then explained Kathy's and his own brief disappearance by saying that autograph seekers had approached her in the ladies' room and he'd positioned himself outside to wait for her.

Everyone seemed to accept the explanation without question. Dinner went on with all the festivity the mayor had intended.

Gib thought he saw something new in Kathy tonight that both enhanced her charisma and alarmed him. She was her usual charming self, fascinating everyone at their table with her wit and intelligence. But there was a new maturity about her, a subtle difference that seemed to draw her just beyond his reach.

She smiled when he spoke to her, but without the wholehearted warmth and mirth he'd grown used to seeing in her eyes. She answered him with her customary attention to honesty and cleverness, but the spark that had once ignited all their conversations was missing.

Two things converged on his awareness. One of them was the photograph of him and Kathy his aunt Rose had clipped out of the paper. It was the one taken on the dance floor in New Orleans. He looked at it again while the mayor escorted Kathy up to a small podium set up in the room.

When Rose had first given it to him, he'd begun to fold it up again without looking at it, thinking that he'd seen it so often, it had nothing new to tell him. Then he'd remembered Rose's question. "Have you seen how she looks at you?"

He'd missed that, he guessed, because he'd been

so startled at first by the naked need for her in his own eyes. He'd thought the photo showed only the back of Kathy, but on closer inspection he saw that though it showed the back of her dress, her profile was visible.

And it was all there in the upswept line of her throat, her chin angled up to him, her lips slightly parted as though she were speaking the words shouting at him from her profile's thickly lashed eye.

It said "I love you," as clearly as if the photo had sound.

The second thing to fill his awareness was the terrible emptiness he'd felt when he'd gotten off the elevator with his aunts on the penthouse floor and discovered that Kathy and Neil had never reached it.

The emptiness was something completely apart from his fear for her safety and his guilt over having done his job badly.

It was the utter vacuum his life would be without her. It was dark and airless and made him feel more alone than the night when he'd been four and had had a nightmare, and no one had come to offer comfort.

The trouble was, he wasn't sure that created an equation. She loved him, and his life was nothing without her. Did that mean he could love her the way she deserved?

Before he could answer his own question, the mayor called everyone's attention to the podium. Reporters had been allowed into the room and now snaked around it in a line, cameras and tape recorders ready.

The mayor welcomed Kathy and her family, introduced Gib's aunts and explained Neil's absence using the excuse Gib had given about the urgent meeting. Then he smiled at Kathy.

"When I first heard Kathryn McQuade, author of *The Virgin Returns,* was coming to Reno on a promotional tour, I thought London Publishing's publicity department had made a strange choice. Reno's a wonderful place to live, but we're mostly about gambling and entertainment.

"Then I was pleasantly surprised to hear my two teenage daughters talking about her book, and realized that she had a good message for them—that if anything shouldn't be a gamble, it was their futures. A good message is a good message anywhere.

"So, again, I'd like to tell Kathy how welcome she is here." He listed the appearances she would make while in town, then turned the microphone over to her for questions.

"What's the announcement, Miss McQuade?" one of the reporters asked immediately. "Representative Barton led us to believe that something significant was happening tonight. And he's gone back to a *budget* meeting?"

Kathy remained poised. Only Gib, who could now read every flutter of her eyelashes, saw that she was upset.

He stood abruptly, and a low buzz of conversation filled the room as he went to join her at the podium. He put an arm around her shoulders, ignoring her look of wary confusion, and took over the microphone.

"The announcement is that Miss McQuade and I are about to be engaged," he said without preamble, keeping a firm grip on Kathy that prevented her start of surprise from being visible to the audience.

Cheers and applause greeted the announcement, along with repeated camera flashes and shouted questions that were indiscernible in the resultant din.

Gib placed a hand over the microphone and turned to Kathy with what he hoped looked like loving words.

''Smile,'' he warned quietly.

She did, but tremulously. Fortunately the crowd probably translated it as happy emotion. ''What are you doing?'' she demanded in a whisper.

''Just back me up,'' he said.

''About to be?'' a female voice from the back of the room asked as the noise quieted.

Kathy almost screamed when Gib pulled a black velvet box out of his breast pocket. The crowd oohed.

He withdrew a simple but giant solitaire on a gold band and slipped it onto her trembling finger. ''Kathryn Victoria McQuade,'' he said clearly and loudly enough to be picked up on all the tape recorders held in their direction, ''will you marry me?''

Kathy didn't really hear the question because her heart was pounding so loudly in her ears she couldn't hear. But she did read his lips.

He's doing this to maintain the tour's momentum, she thought in a kind of panic-induced trance. To save the house for his aunts. To save his own income. Or maybe just to allow her to save face.

All of those reasons fell short of what she wanted. She couldn't say yes to them.

But when she saw the crowd rise to its feet, applauding, as though in some silent movie, her mother weeping and Jack smiling, she realized that she must have.

Then Gib's head came down to block out her sight, as well, and all she could do was feel his arms wrap around her and crush her to him as his mouth opened over hers.

She maintained a thin grip on sanity by realizing that this moment in time could not be real.

"WHAT IN THE NAME of all that's holy did you think you were doing?" Kathy demanded.

She and Gib were alone in the back of the limo. The mayor had driven Patsy and Jack back to the hotel, insisting with an understanding wink that Kathy and Gib have the limo to themselves.

The aunts had walked their nephew and his fiancée to the limo in a flurry of coos and congratulations. Only Cordelia gave the firm line of Kathy's mouth a second look and suspected something was amiss. "Your parents had difficulty finding love," she whispered to Gib, "but they certainly believed in it, because they looked so hard for it. Don't give up, Gilbert."

Kathy sat across from him in the facing seat, suddenly more frazzled than he'd ever seen her. He found a curious comfort in that.

"I thought I was pretty clear," he said, his legs stretched out to the side of hers. She was all tucked up under herself as though she were trying to shrink. "I proposed marriage. You accepted."

"I...didn't."

"You did. It's on tape. And by tomorrow morning it's going to be in every newspaper headline and on every radio and television newscast."

"Well, you'd havc looked pretty silly if Neil had proposed to me, as well!"

He grinned. "I knew I wasn't going to let that happen. I did have a friend in Boston check to see if the budget committee had met while we were in Phoenix. If they had, and you wanted to marry him, he might have been a better risk for you than I would be. But he lied. I, at least, am honest."

"Are you?" She folded her arms and glowered at him. "You proposed to me to save the tour," she accused.

He shook his head. "That'll be a result, I'm sure, but that isn't why I did it."

"You did it to save the house for your aunts."

He sighed and looked out the window at the passing storefronts, casinos and late-night revelers. It was painful, he thought, to finally declare your love for someone and have them doubt your honesty and your motives.

Then he remembered that he'd done just that to her countless times, yet she hadn't given up on him. Until today.

No. She could not have given up. It couldn't happen. His world couldn't go on if she had.

God. Love, he reflected, was a lot like business, in that timing was everything.

He forced himself to remain calm, because she didn't seem to be, and he was going to have to save this relationship singlehandedly. Him. The love neophyte.

"My aunts' home is secure," he told Kathy. "Since I've been taking care of the company's finances this past year, I've dabbled in theirs, too, without their knowledge. I paid off the mortgage they took out to keep the business afloat a couple of years ago. The payments they think they're making on it go into a special account for their retirement."

"But...why?"

"Because they like working together for a purpose," he replied, "and they'd be pretty upset with me if they knew I'd done that. So, no harm done."

"Then you were trying to save your own..." She seemed to be losing confidence in her latest argument.

"My own stake in the business?" he finished for her. "No. Sorry. I have a couple of million. I'm good with money."

Her eyes were the size of saucers. Her lips were trembling. "A couple of—"

"Yes. Any more arguments you'd like to offer?"

She just stared at him.

"Then what's the logical reason left to us?" He leaned toward her, elbows on his knees. "You're a smart woman. Think."

She did. Lights from Commercial Row flickered through the dark interior of the limo, illuminating her blue eyes. Unfortunately, they did not also illuminate her thoughts.

"I don't know," she said finally. "But I'm sure love doesn't just happen. Particularly when you've denied the possibility of its existence all this time."

He leaned back with an exasperated sigh. "How do you think it happens?" he asked. "How did you decide you loved me?"

She seemed taken aback by the question. "I don't know! It started with interest, I think." She frowned, concentrating. "You were obstinate and difficult, but that day in Denver when the boys were in my closet. It was—" she sighed "—it was wonderful when you held me. And I felt as though I could stay in your arms forever.''

He swallowed, tortured by that memory and the possibility that he wasn't going to be able to change her mind.

''I guess,'' he said, ''that this has been my point all along. You had love and knew what to do with interest and trust in someone. I didn't. I was afraid of it. But I'm not anymore.''

She met his eyes, her own suspicious. He didn't flinch.

Then she looked down at the ring on her finger and gave it a turn. ''When did you buy this?''

''Today. In the jewelry store on the street floor of our hotel, right after I got the word that Neil had lied about the meeting.''

She studied it a moment, then pulled it off and tried to hand it back to him.

His heart twisted, but he pushed the ring back to her. ''You have to wear it. The whole world knows we're engaged.''

She clutched it in her fist and frowned at him. There was pain and confusion in her eyes. ''Until the tour's over. Then it's all off.''

''Says you.''

''I'm an important part of the equation!'' she pointed out indignantly. ''If I don't want to get married, you can't make me.''

Not believing that he loved her weighed heavily inside her like something made of iron. She could see over and around it to the life they could have had together, the life she'd dreamed of. But she couldn't push her way through the obstruction of her own doubt.

He leaned toward her again, his eyes suddenly weary. "You know what I think is wrong with you?" he asked.

She looked away. "I'm sure you have a long list."

"Actually, I don't," he said. "I've known a lot of women in my time, and you're about as close to perfect for a lifetime companion as I've ever seen."

She turned her head slowly toward him, almost afraid of what would follow that compliment.

"The problem," he said, "is that you're a virgin."

She was about to explode, taking that remark at face value. But he raised a placating hand. "No. Not because you have no sexual experience. But because being naked with someone leaves you very little to hide behind and you're faced with the truth that life is messy. If you'd ever been with someone, you might know that.

"You want love to be some vast emotional experience through which you feel cherished and adored and never doubt its depth or its longevity. Now you don't believe it can come from some jerk who couldn't even recognize it until you walked into his life, then didn't know what to do with it when you offered it.

"You want it to be as pure as you are. You don't want it cluttered with doubt or confusion or mistakes." He leaned back again, both hands raised in surrender. "I'm sorry. I can't give you anything that clean. Physically, I've been around, but this is the first time I've given my heart. And I'll tell you. Giving your body is easier."

Chapter Thirteen

Her life was over, but the tour wasn't. Kathy confronted that truth by going from one appearance to another in the realization that though she'd completely sabotaged her personal life, she'd learned over the past month what it took to be a professional.

She just had to learn to be one on her own.

She'd always believed that the purpose of celibacy was to finally be able to share every particle of your most intimate self, physically and spiritually, with the person for whom you'd preserved it.

Clearly—in her own practice of it, at least—she'd done something terribly wrong.

GIB WAS AMAZED to learn that love could still burn like a torch inside, even when the object of that love didn't return it. Or worse, didn't believe in it.

It was only then that he finally understood what the fuss was all about. Why everyone went to the ends of the earth and through partner after partner trying to find it.

That was also the point at which Kathy's theory began to make sense to him.

He knew the physical power of sex, but had always denied that it had anything to do with a lifelong commitment.

Now that he loved her, all he thought about was making love to her—and not because of what it would do for him, but because of what he wanted her to experience. And though he'd always had sex before and had never actually "made love," he knew he would do it well because the love inside him was so deep, so profound, that it made a difference to everything he knew and felt. It would have to make a difference when he took her to his bed.

But she seemed determined not to allow him that privilege.

What he felt, however, was too big to let him consider giving in to defeat. He hung his hopes on the next three days in L.A. He didn't know how he was going to change her mind, he just knew he had to.

BY THE END of their second day in Los Angeles, Kathy had been on three radio shows, made four television appearances and done a book signing at Pickwick. She was asked to show off her ring, recount the tale of the night of her engagement and share her honeymoon plans and their dreams for the future.

Gib's aunts, who'd accompanied them to L.A. and taken an adjoining suite, were aware of the unhappiness between them despite the public image. Cordelia had pleaded with Kathy not to dismiss her and Gib's future plans as "undecided" when she was interviewed.

"Give details," she had advised. "That's the only

way to be convincing.'' Then she'd smiled slyly. ''And it might even reveal something to you about what you really want out of your life. Having experienced celibacy for a lifetime, dear, I assure you there are preferable goals.''

So Kathy had provided detail out of her imagination. A honeymoon on Capri, a house on a hill in Bayside, a career as a mystery novelist, four children that looked like Gib.

In the dark of night, she lay alone and sleepless in the enormous expanse of bed and cried over Cordelia's wisdom.

GIB ANSWERED A KNOCK on the door of their hotel suite the morning of their last day in Los Angeles. Patsy and Jack had taken Gib's aunts to visit Universal Studios. Kathy, exhausted, had chosen to stay behind.

Gib, despite her protests, stayed also, reminding her that she'd shut him out of her heart, but he was still her bodyguard.

She'd closed herself in her room to rest for their appearance tonight on ''Larry Duke Live.'' The much-married talk-show host had been touched by their story and invited both of them on his show.

Gib had wanted to decline, at least for himself, but everyone in their party had risen up in arms, so he'd finally accepted.

He'd been brewing a pot of coffee when he'd heard the knock.

A tall man Gib guessed to be his own age, wearing glasses and a three-piece suit, stood on the other side of the door.

''You must be Gib London,'' the man said.

Gib nodded.

"I'm Grant Miller." He offered his hand, his expression chagrined. "My son, Justin, and his friend were in Miss McQuade's closet..."

"Oh, yes." Gib shook his hand, puzzled by his presence. "But don't you live in Denver?"

Miller nodded, his expression now very apologetic. "I do, but I'm a salesman for a software firm, and I travel a lot. At least I used to. I just took an office job. My son, I realize, needs more of my attention."

Gib couldn't fault a father who came to that conclusion, since his own father never had. He invited him inside.

"I just got in last night, and when I saw in the paper that Miss McQuade was in L.A., I had to stop by and apologize in person for Justin's intrusion. It was generous of you not to call the police. Or even the hotel authorities."

Gib pointed him to a sofa near the open doors that led to a covered patio. "I was convinced they meant no harm. I think a dare from the other kids..."

Miller nodded away the excuse. "Yes. But you hope you've raised your kids to resist dares and think first. Particularly when it had the potential to hurt someone else. Is Miss McQuade in?"

Gib opened his mouth to explain that she was asleep, when she walked into the room, her hand extended toward Miller, who stood to greet her.

She was wearing pale yellow cotton slacks and a matching shirt, and her hair was tied up in a loose knot. She looked drowsy and soft, and Gib had to look away to prevent himself from reaching out to her.

"Hi, Mr. Miller," she said warmly. "I was just getting up and overheard some of your conversation. The boys scared me to death, but I know they meant no harm. It was thoughtful of you to come by, but completely unnecessary."

"I thought it necessary," he insisted. "I'm frankly horrified that a kid of mine did something like that, and I wanted you to know he's not bad, just young enough to be thoughtless."

Kathy nodded. "I understand. He and his friend were very apologetic when they were discovered."

"I was explaining to Mr. London that my job required that I travel a lot, but my wife died a year ago and my being gone so much wasn't working, even though Justin would stay with my brother. So I've taken an office job. The only unfortunate thing is that it's in Manhattan."

Kathy smiled. "Oh, we were in Manhattan for just a couple of days, and I thought it was wonderful. I bet you'll love it."

"I'm sure we will." He pushed himself to his feet. "As soon as we make some friends. Justin's both excited and terrified."

Gib stood, also, and felt the lightning bolt of sudden inspiration.

He turned to Kathy and saw the same expression in her eyes. "Andrea?" she asked him.

He nodded. "You have her phone number?"

"Excuse me." Kathy skirted the coffee table and disappeared into her room.

"We have a friend in New York," Gib explained to Miller, thinking that those few words were the first time he and Kathy had really communicated in three days. "She's a little lonely, too. I'm sure she'd enjoy helping you learn your way around."

Miller's eyes brightened. "Well, thank you."

Kathy returned with Andrea's business card.

Miller studied it, then smiled at Gib, then Kathy. "I guess what they say is true."

"What's that?" Kathy asked.

"That people who've found love are always trying to pair up other people." He shook hands and thanked them one more time. They walked him to the door.

As Gib closed the door behind Miller, Kathy smiled thinly. "I'll enjoy thinking about him and Justin and Andrea going to dinner somewhere overlooking Central Park."

Gib nodded. "Yeah. Me, too."

Kathy sniffed the air suddenly, then walked into the small kitchen. "No coffee brewing?" she teased. "You're slipping."

He pointed to the packet of coffee he'd left on the counter when he'd answered the door. "I was just about to make some when Miller came."

She picked up the packet and read the flavor. "Caramel vanilla."

"Not my style," he said, "but I knew you'd be up soon."

She ripped open the packet and filled the coffeemaker's basket with it. "That was very thoughtful."

"It's the gesture of a man in love."

Her easy manner changed in a heartbeat, and she gave him a quick, frowning glance. "Not today, Gib."

"You think it's going to go away if you refuse to deal with it?"

She shoved the basket in place in the coffeemaker and turned impatiently to him. "That always worked for *you,* didn't it?"

He shook his head. "Apparently not. We're still in love."

She took the empty carafe off the warming plate. "You're not in love. I'm probably the only woman you've spent this much time with without having sex, and you've confused love with the need to—"

He snatched the pot from her and slapped it onto the counter as anger shot up in him like a fireworks finale. Even he was surprised the glass didn't break.

"Yes, I am desperate to have you," he said tightly, looking into her stubborn expression and wondering why his discovery of love after so long had to come in such a difficult package. "But don't get righteous with me. You've badgered me constantly, when I didn't *want* to love you. You've given me those looks that would melt metal, you climbed into my bed, bringing all my fantasies to life, and you tried to get me to make love to you just to prove the point that I wouldn't be able to let you do it!"

KATHY WAS NOW backed into a corner of the counter. He had a hand on the counter on one side of her, and one extended to the cabinet at her shoulder level on the other. She had no place to go.

He leaned over her until she was forced to inch away. She was aware of her heart pounding, and her breath lodged somewhere in her chest. She didn't seem to be able to fill her lungs.

"But you were right, weren't you?" His voice had a cold, quiet edge to it that raised the gooseflesh on her arms. "I couldn't take what you offered because I was finally beginning to understand what you've been talking about. I saw what was growing between us as something precious that did need special care and treatment so that when it was finally time for us to give it life, we'd be in just the right place—the doorway to a future we'd promised to spend together."

He paused, putting a hand to his chest. She was too trapped by his words to realize that she had a way out.

"I've been absolutely *heroic,*" he said with no pretensions of modesty, "in keeping my passion and desire for you in check, so don't you *dare* belittle it by telling me it's all I want."

And then he closed his arms around her and kissed the life out of her. She could feel the power of what he felt in his arms, in the body against which she was pressed. But every touch of his hands and mouth was tender—expressing love.

He raised his head after a long moment and drew a ragged breath. "I've got to get away from you," he said, pushing himself out of her grasp, because she was now holding him as though he was a lifeline in a vast and empty ocean. "Don't leave the room. I'll be back in a few minutes."

It wasn't until she heard the door close behind him that she recovered her senses sufficiently to feel the loss. She made herself pick up the carafe again and fill it with water, pour the water into the reservoir, then turn on the pot. She reached in an overhead cupboard for a cup and pulled it down.

Then as the coffee began to brew, she caught a

whiff of the caramel-vanilla blend and reality hit her on the head like a rubber mallet.

Idiot! Of course he loves you! What's wrong with you? Was your pursuit of him just a game so that when you finally caught him, you didn't know what to do with him?

"No," she responded aloud to herself. "It was just such an uphill struggle that when he finally admitted he loved me, I couldn't believe it was real. I mean, he's so special. Look at what he's been through and still he learned to love me."

Her heart thumping, her breath finally returning, but in gasps, Kathy ran to the door to call him back.

She was confused when the door seemed to fling her backward. She stood several feet from it, staring at it in confusion, when she realized that everything else in the room—and under her feet—was rattling, bouncing, moving.

An earthquake!

She heard a cry of surprise in the hallway, something crashing to the floor in the kitchen, the musical banging together of crockery.

Oh, God! she thought, holding on to the sofa as everything shook. *I finally realize that I can't live another moment without being Gib London's wife, on the very day that Los Angeles has "The Big One"?*

And then, as quickly as it had begun, the shaking stopped.

Kathy waited a moment to be sure it was over, then yanked the door open. This time it didn't fight back. Two women from housekeeping were picking up towels that had fallen off a cart.

"Did you see a tall man?" Kathy asked as she

bent to help. "He came out of this room just before the shaking started."

Both shook their heads. One of them smiled kindly and put a calming hand to her arm. "It's all right. That was just a tremor."

Kathy nodded apologetically. "I'm from Massachusetts. I'm used to hurricanes, but this was my first earthquake." She went around them to the elevators, trying to remember what she'd heard about elevators and earthquakes. They stopped automatically? Was Gib caught somewhere between floors?

Presumably they were stopped for safety's sake, but had he plunged eleven floors before the safety mechanism kicked in?

All right, she told herself, calm down. That's a ridiculous thought. The housekeeper had been right. It was just a tremor. Nothing had happened to the elevator.

But her fears refused to be calmed. It hadn't been that bad, but that was just the kind of tragedy that befell people who struggle to find love, then finally have it within their grasp. It's stolen from them by a cruel fate that doesn't believe in happy endings.

It's—

"Kathy!" The authoritative shout of her name was followed by the sound of running footsteps. "Kathy?"

She ran back to the suite just as Gib ran out of the open door.

"Gib!" she called, and flew into his arms.

He caught her and crushed her to him, lifting her clear of the carpet. He walked back into the suite with her held against him and put her down just inside. "Are you all right?" he asked urgently. He held her at arm's length and turned her hands over, as though looking for injury. "I found the coffee-maker and hot water all over the kitchen floor."

She went back into his arms. "I'm fine," she said, holding him tightly. "I thought you were stuck in the elevator."

He rubbed a hand gently up and down her spine. "I had to cool off, so I took the stairs."

There was a moment of complete silence, then the mood of joyous reunion was broken by the return of the tension that had lived between them since the night of the party in Reno. He took a step back from her, his expression carefully blank. "I'll clean up the kitchen."

She opened her mouth to stop him, but she didn't seem able to string the right words together. It struck her as ironic that she, who had a bestselling book, couldn't find the words.

She followed him into the kitchen. "I'll help you," she said. Those words came easily because they weren't the ones she wanted.

"You're supposed to be resting for tonight." He turned to point her back to the bedroom. "I can handle it."

She stopped abruptly, just in time to avoid his pointing finger. "I want to help."

The last thing Gib wanted at this moment was to be confined with her in the small space of the kitchen. When he'd raced back upstairs after the tremor, and she'd flown into his arms, he had his life's desire.

Then he realized that fear had propelled her there and not love. So he had to let go or he never would.

He tried to look firm. "I don't need your help. Just let me handle it."

He turned to the task, thinking his words would spark her temper and she'd stalk away. Instead, she walked around the mess to get a small wastebasket out from under the sink.

He got down on his haunches with a wad of paper towels and sopped up water, pushing the shattered glass toward the middle of the puddle.

"Oh, yeah?" she challenged in the taunting and playful tone he remembered from the first few days of the tour. "Well, I think you do. When I first met you, you were a playboy who didn't believe in love. Now look at you." She got down beside him and reached for a large piece of glass to put it in the basket.

He caught her wrist and met her eyes, suspicious of her motives in bringing that up. He put her hand aside and reached for the glass himself. "Now I'm a bodyguard and love doesn't believe in *me*. You're suggesting there's been improvement somewhere?"

"Yes. Well...maybe."

"That's clear." He dropped all the larger pieces of glass into the basket and collected most of the small ones in the now-soggy towel.

Kathy stood, yanked four towels off the roll and dampened them. Then she handed them to him. "I mean, *you* might not consider it an improvement."

He looked up at her. "Thank you. Why not?"

"Because I love you. Because I believe you love me."

Certain his brain had stopped functioning, he dropped the towels over what remained of the puddle and pushed to his feet. She was studying him with watchful uncertainty. His heartbeat was picking up.

"What?" he asked simply.

"I love you," she repeated, her voice raspy, the words quick. "Maybe the earthquake shook sense into me. You weren't there and I thought you were on the elevator and that maybe it fell...." The earlier fear she'd felt was renewed in her eyes and her voice. Her hands began to tremble.

He took them in his to calm her. But his heartbeat began to quicken at her admission and he wondered who would calm him. "Okay. I can't tell you what it does for me to hear that. But...that wasn't the problem. You didn't believe that I..."

"I know!" Her eyes filled with tears. "Wasn't that the stupidest thing? I think you were right about my perception of love. I thought it clarified everything, purified everything, so that when someone finally would give it to me, I'd be this wise Wonder Woman who would be perfect from that moment on." Her eyes implored him to understand. "But when I still felt like myself—maybe even a little more confused than usual—hearing you tell me you loved me was suddenly a responsibility that frightened me. What if I couldn't be as good at loving as I thought I could be? I've never been very domestic. What if I made a poor wife? And then—" she swallowed and added with a little embarrassed hitch of her shoulder "—what if I wasn't any good at making love?"

He opened his mouth to disabuse her of all those concerns, but she shook her head and pinched his fingers. "Please let me finish. I have to tell you what I figured out."

Happiness was like a supernova in his chest. It had to have release or he was going to explode. "Okay. But hurry up. I have an uncontrollable urge to hold you."

She smiled at him hopefully. "You do? You haven't given up?"

He still held her hands and now laced his fingers in hers. "No. I haven't. You were saying?"

"That love doesn't clean up your life," she explained, her eyes reflecting the wonder of that discovery, "it just makes it possible to live with the confusion and the imperfection. When everything was shaking, I was wishing desperately that you were here, not to protect me, but just because I feel better when you're with me."

She smiled widely at him, her eyes clear. "That's it," she said. "You can hold me now."

He swept her up into his arms and carried her into the living room where he sat on the sofa with her and kissed her until neither of them could breathe.

They were staring at each other, lost for words, when Patsy and Jack burst through the suite door, followed by Cordelia, Lucinda and Rose.

"Oh!" Patsy exclaimed in surprise at their cozy embrace. "We, um, wanted to make sure you were okay. I mean, it wasn't much of a quake, I guess, but, ah, well—"

"I think they're fine," Jack said, pulling Patsy back out into the hallway. "We'll go get a cup of coffee or something. What do you say, ladies? Will you join us?"

"No, thank you," Rose said wistfully, taking a step into the room. "I'd like to stay and watch."

"Honestly!" Lucinda caught her arm and pulled her into the hall. "You kids just carry on."

"But not too far," Cordelia warned in a whisper loud enough to draw a laugh from Jack as well as Gib. Then the door closed behind her, and Gib and Kathy were alone again.

Gib found that his memories of loneliness and neglect had been erased. He felt whole and—despite intimate knowledge to the contrary—perfect. "We're getting married next Saturday in Bayside," he said as she lay contentedly against his shoulder, her arms around his neck.

"That sounds wonderful."

"We'll honeymoon in Capri, build that house on the hill, and start working on the kids."

She stretched like a happy cat. "Four."

"Right. And an awful lot of yellow puppies."

She sat up suddenly to look into his eyes, and the love he saw in hers rendered him speechless. She kissed him fiercely, then fell against him again. "Thank you," she whispered. "Thank you, thank you."

"I love the way you express gratitude," he said, stroking her hair. "But, for what? You're the one who gave life to me."

"For letting me love you. For not objecting when I brought back the puppies. For being everything I ever wanted and needed."

"Well, that remains to be seen, but—my pleasure." He kissed her ear, then sighed at how slowly the time would pass until Saturday. "I can't wait to let you *make* love to me. And I'm sure you're going to be inspired and brilliant at it."

She raised her head again to smile into his eyes. "How do you know?"

He looked into her beautiful face and was humbly astonished at the turn his life had taken. "Because," he said, wondering how he knew this, when, in a way, he was as much a virgin as she was, "all your body has to do is translate what's in your heart."

Epilogue

"I'm going to be sick," Gib threatened in a whisper to Kathy as they sat at the oak table where Larry Duke would join them in a moment. There were cameras, lights and microphones everywhere.

Kathy tucked her arm in Gib's, feeling surprisingly serene. She was going to spend the rest of her life with Gib London. She felt invincible.

"It's going to be fine," she said, squeezing his arm. "I'll talk about the book and he'll probably just ask you about us. That'll be easy to talk about."

He smiled suddenly, the love in his eyes pushing aside the stage fright. "You think so? I'm not sure I'll be able to find words big enough."

"Hi! I'm Larry Duke." A tall, lean, gray-haired man took his place at the table and someone hurried over to fit them with minute microphones clipped to the front of their clothes.

Then someone was counting down, music played, and Duke began speaking to the camera, telling his viewers about tonight's show.

He indicated Gib and Kathy. "And, of course, by now you're all familiar with the country's most famous virgin, Kathryn McQuade, and her bodyguard,

Gib London, who are soon to become Mr. and Mrs. Was that an earthquake today, kids, or did your love make the earth move?''

Gib watched, his heart full, as Kathy laughed in response. ''We didn't cause it,'' she said with a wink at Gib. ''But we did benefit from it. Everyone has to be shaken up once in a while to remember to hold on to each other.''

''Tell us about the tour,'' Duke said, leaning toward them companionably. ''Who'd have thought that encouraging young women to abstain from sex would have earned you such a loud and supportive following? Why do you think that is?''

''I'm not entirely sure,'' Kathy replied, ''but it might be that when I began this tour, it was because my life and my future were important to me. But the more women I met, the more young people I saw, *their* lives became important to me. I want them to be protected and cared about. I want them to wait for what they deserve to have in a life partner.''

After more discussion and several phoned-in contributions to the subject, Duke suddenly smiled. ''Now I'd like you to meet some other friends Kathy and Gib made along the way. Please bring Sam out. Sam Sheffield was Kathy's chauffeur while she and her mother and Gib were in Denver. He was entrusted with the care of these *friends.*''

Kathy gasped as Sam came on stage holding five leashes attached to five beribboned Golden Retriever puppies. Kathy leapt out of her chair to embrace Sam and to greet the puppies. They jumped all over her in tail-wagging excitement.

Gib watched the camera back away to get a wide

shot of him and Duke talking while keeping Kathy, Sam, and the puppies in the frame.

As Kathy tried to take the leashes from Sam, one pup escaped and ran toward the table. Gib pushed his chair back to scoop him up and surfaced again with the puppy frantically licking his chin.

Duke smiled sympathetically at Gib. ''You're a decorated hero, respected editor, and now an officer in the family publishing company.'' He pointed with fondness but amused concern at Kathy and the pups. ''What is this woman and her unorthodox ideas going to do to the rest of your life?''

Kathy looked at Gib as the puppies ran around her, completely immobilizing her in a tangle of leashes. Laughing, she stretched a hand out to him.

He had to draw a steadying breath to be able to speak. ''I don't have a clue. But I can't wait to find out,'' he replied as he tucked the puppy into the crook of his arm and went to her.

COMING NEXT MONTH

#773 ONE HOT DADDY-TO-BE? by Judy Christenberry
4 Tots for 4 Texans
Nothing is more important for four elderly mothers of Cactus, Texas, than making their sons fathers. They're not even above a little bet...so the baby race is on! Bachelor #1, Cal Baxter, never knew he'd one day be looking at his childhood friend Jessica Hoya as a prospective mother of his child...but he never knew how determined his mother could be!

#774 THE LAST TWO BACHELORS by Linda Randall Wisdom
Delaney's Grooms
"You've just seen your new mother." The prophetic note that ring bearer Patric pulls out of his tux pocket tells him he and his dad, Jack O'Connor, have a prospect for a new wife and mom...but how could that be, when she's the beautiful woman trying on a wedding gown?

#775 THE ACCIDENTAL MRS. MACKENZIE by Bonnie K. Winn
Brynn Magee had imagined herself to be Douglas MacKenzie's bride for months. But when his family suddenly mistakes her for his real-life bride, she realizes she's in love with Matt MacKenzie—the "groom's" brother!

#776 FATHER IN TRAINING by Mollie Molay
New Arrivals
It was one of those things: a moonlit night, an incredibly sexy guy, music in the background. Before she knew what happened, Abby Carson was in the arms of the man she'd been wishing for all her life. But now, was Jeff Logan ready to be a daddy?